"Is there any part of your life that you don't organize and control?" Sam asked.

"Ever had an impulse you *didn't* act on?" Clare shot back before she could stop herself.

His long slow smile took her breath away. "Some of my favorite impulses are the ones I don't act on. Waiting is sometimes half the fun. Think about it. Anticipation and foreplay. One's mental. One's physical. Together they're mind-blowing."

Sensing her withdrawal, Sam twisted her own words and asked, "Ever had an impulse you *did* act on?"

Clare's chin came up. "Not that I'm particularly proud of."

"Well, at least you admit to having impulses."

"Are you done?" Clare asked, refusing the bait and eyeing the door. Without words, she made her desire to leave very plain.

Sam scooted his chair back and watched her graceful exit. But when the door clicked softly behind her, he promised, "Lady, I'm just getting started."

WHAT ARE *LOVESWEPT* ROMANCES?

They are stories of true romance and touching emotion. We believe those two very important ingredients are constants in our highly sensual and very believable stories in the LOVE-SWEPT line. Our goal is to give you, the reader, stories of consistently high quality that may sometimes make you laugh, sometimes make you cry, but are always fresh and creative and contain many delightful surprises within their pages.

Most romance fans read an enormous number of books. Those they truly love, they keep. Others may be traded with friends and soon forgotten. We hope that each LOVESWEPT romance will be a treasure—a "keeper." We will always try to publish

LOVE STORIES YOU'LL NEVER FORGET
BY AUTHORS YOU'LL ALWAYS REMEMBER

The Editors

Loveswept ® 781

SLOW
HANDS

DEBRA
DIXON

BANTAM BOOKS
NEW YORK · TORONTO · LONDON · SYDNEY · AUCKLAND

SLOW HANDS
A Bantam Book / March 1996

ISBN 0-553-44397-6

Published simultaneously in the United States and Canada

Bantam Books are published by Bantam Books, a division of Bantam Dou-
bleday Dell Publishing Group, Inc. Its trademark, consisting of the words
"Bantam Books" and the portrayal of a rooster, is Registered in U.S. Patent
and Trademark Office and in other countries. Marca Registrada. Bantam
Books, 1540 Broadway, New York, New York 10036.

PRINTED IN THE UNITED STATES OF AMERICA

OPM   0 9 8 7 6 5 4 3 2 1

My heartfelt thanks to a couple of
people who've waited a long time to
see this book in print—

Sandra Chastain,
a wonderful southern lady
who helped the dream come true

Joyce Flaherty,
who kept the magic going

ONE

Sam Tucker slung a hip onto the edge of his cluttered desk and looked at the expectant faces. For a moment he enjoyed the almost silent intake of breath as the perfectly pressed group of corporate executives realized their careers rested in his hands. To be honest, Sam doubted his shaggy blond hair, or the frayed slits in the knees of his jeans, scared the class half as much as the incredible mountain of chaos on his desk.

That chaos represented exactly what each of these people feared most—letting the paperwork pile up, losing control. As a result, all fifteen of them looked at him in varying degrees of horror, wondering what he could possibly teach them and why they were meeting in the converted carriage house of a restored Victorian mansion. Especially since the ivy-covered college that offered the unique course was only a few blocks away. Sam imagined some of them were even wondering if it was too late to get their money back.

"Welcome to Losing Control of Your Life," Sam said with a broad smile. "For those of you who still harbor some hope that you might be in the wrong place, you're not. This is indeed the first session of the Executive Burnout series. I'm Sam Tucker, and I'm going to teach you how to have some fun."

As soon as the woman raised her hand, Sam knew instinctively who she was and that his old friend Dave Gronski had set him up. Just that morning Dave had called, asking for a favor. The class was full, and he wanted Sam to pull some strings to get his controller in. He swore the woman was overworked and at the end of a very short rope. He swore that she needed this class. He swore Sam wouldn't be sorry.

Oh, yes, Dave had told him everything about Ms. Clare McGuire—except that she had incredible legs, eyes to die for, and an abundance of short, sassy blue-black hair. Dave owed him a case of very old scotch for neglecting to tell him that organized, punctual, precise Clare McGuire was everything he'd want and nothing he'd need.

"Yes, Clare," he said, and tried not to narrow his eyes or stare at her legs.

Startled, Clare snatched her hand down as everyone swiveled to look at her. *How the hell did he know who she was!* Dave, of course. Dave must have given him a description. *Probably wanted to be sure I didn't pay someone to take this damn class for me!*

Not that she hadn't thought about it. Especially when she walked through the carriage house door a few moments before and entered a time warp. The place reminded her of an English lord's library, full of musty books and the glow of lovingly polished wood. For a second Clare had even imagined the fruity aroma of pipe smoke. Some sort of cherry tobacco. And then she'd found a seat and reminded herself that she wasn't there to enjoy the atmosphere.

Regaining her composure, Clare folded her hands in her lap and posed her question. "Having fun is a nice concept, but isn't fun entirely subjective? I mean, how can you *grade* fun?"

"Is that the only reason you're here? To add another management course to your résumé?" Sam couldn't resist asking even though he knew exactly why she was there. Her job depended on passing his course. Dave had given her an ultimatum—loosen up or lose the job. Profits were up in the auto parts company, but so was employee turnover.

Sam didn't wait for an answer. Instead, he leaned forward, challenging her. "Is there anything wrong with just having fun?"

"Yes," Clare said bluntly, and decided she didn't much like Sam Tucker. She raised an eyebrow and added, "Having fun generally gets in the way of taking care of business."

Her eyes focused on his messy desk in silent accusation, but he didn't explain. If she had *asked* about the mess, he might have told her about the locksmith creating chaos when he took the antique file cabinet to the shop for repairs. But she didn't ask. She raised an eyebrow and looked smug. So he didn't explain.

"What about the rest of you?" Sam transferred his attention to the remainder of the class seated in comfortable chairs scattered about the room in a loose semicircle. "What's your opinion of fun?"

"It's been so long, I've forgotten what it is!" said a

sincere young woman. A chorus of agreement echoed through the carriage house.

Sam sympathized. Two years earlier he'd felt the same way. He remembered having the same tired bags beneath his eyes as most of them did now. Workaholics missed life and died young.

"Then let me define fun," he told them, "because over the next six weeks you're going to learn how to relax and have some. Fun is something you do for yourself because it feels good."

He paused and fanned another gaze around the room. "You can't analyze it. You can't plan it. You can't execute it on a tight schedule. And that's what you people are here to learn. Fun is a moment you seize because it's there."

Clare settled back, wondering if she could last six weeks without seizing Tucker's neck and strangling him. Now, that might be fun. If she had time for fun, which she didn't. She was already three weeks behind on the analysis of the past year's budget deviations. The new computer system was scheduled for installation in two weeks. Her temporary *male* secretary couldn't find a dictionary, much less spell. And her cousin Ellie was coming for a—how did she phrase it?—"long overdue sisterly visit." *Inspection* was more accurate.

And what was she going to tell Ellie? *Glad you finally found time to visit after five years, and by the way, I lied about everything I told you in my letters?* Slowly Clare loosened her grip on her day planner and forced herself to concentrate on the wave of laughter that rippled through the room.

The longer Tucker talked, Clare noted, the more the group relaxed. One woman unbent long enough to give him a come-hither look with her eyes, but the man was either unaware of the patently sexual invitation or petite redheads weren't his type. Since Clare didn't think a blind man could have mistaken the lustful stare, she decided Tucker liked his women taller and blonder. Most men did. Most men liked Ellie.

Of course, Ellie liked most men. Especially men as undeniably attractive as Tucker. What's not to like? Clare asked herself. His carelessly tousled blond hair? The way he raked his hand through it as he passionately explained the mechanics of fun? Or the way his long, muscular thighs filled out his jeans?

His jeans. Clare frowned as she looked at the frayed openings that bared masculine flesh. Why should the sight of strong, tan knees make her swallow? Cutting holes in perfectly good jeans was a stupid waste of money. Regardless of how sexy it might be.

Get a grip, Clare. You don't know the man. Why should you care how he spends his money or if his knees are sexy!

"Clare!" Sam rounded on her with surprising speed.

"Tucker," Clare shot back, hoping she could recover the thread of the conversation before the man realized she hadn't heard a word he said. As soon as she answered, laughter erupted again. Clare straightened. "What?"

"We're choosing research partners," Sam explained helpfully. "Didn't you know that when you said my name? Don't bother to count. We have an uneven number of students enrolled in this class. That means one lucky camper is stuck with me. And I guess since you weren't paying attention, and since you were the last one to sign up, that lucky camper is going to be you."

"Lucky me," Clare forced out, and gave him her best imitation of a smile. Knowing the situation was her own fault didn't erase any of her irritation. Tucker acted as if he'd set a trap and was quite pleased with himself for having caught a fool. *Well, didn't he?* her stubbornly fair subconscious asked.

Sam stifled a chuckle and watched as the rest of the class divided into pairs and rearranged themselves accordingly. With the exception of his "problem child," the rest of the students seemed genuinely interested in learning how to let go of the grind and find their lives again. Not all of them would succeed, but most of them would at least escape the pressure of their lives for a few hours a week.

"Everybody got a partner? Good. Who brought their day planner?" Everyone's hand went up. "That's what I thought," drawled Sam. "Don't bring them to the field trip this weekend and don't bring them to class next week. Who knows a good place for ice cream?"

Velcro crackled as they all pulled open their day planners and turned dutifully to their address indexes for "ice cream." Sam rolled his eyes. This was going to be more difficult than he'd thought.

"People. People! Ice cream is an adventure. Fun usually starts with an adventure. And adventures aren't neatly labeled and penciled in under the appropriate letter of the alphabet."

"Wrong," Clare corrected him suddenly, feeling an unfamiliar urge to one-up Sam Tucker. She recrossed her legs and propped an elbow on her thigh. "*Everyone* knows that adventure, in fact, does begin with an appropriate letter of the alphabet."

Caught off guard, Sam stared at her. "Is that right?"

"Of course." Leaning forward, she enlightened him.

"Any self-respecting adventure begins with X marks the spot."

Pleasantly surprised, he chuckled along with the rest of the class. In the last half hour, Sam had imagined many things about Clare, but not that she possessed a sense of humor. "I stand corrected. Good job, Clare. Less than an hour and you've already made your first joke. See how easy it is? If you're not careful, you might actually enjoy this class.

"Now for the rest of you. I'm cutting tonight short because I want you to take your partner out for coffee. Do me a favor and choose a well-lit public place. Discuss ice cream, your lives, and why you're in this class. And while you're doing all that discussing, take a good look at your partner. You'll be looking in a mirror. Decide whether or not you like what you see. And, people"— Sam slammed his hands together in a thunderous clap— "leave your day planners in the car. Live dangerously. Improvise. Write your partner's name and address on a napkin."

He waved them out the door. "I'll see you Saturday morning. Ten o'clock. We'll go searching for the best ice cream parlor in town."

A few students came up to ask questions, but most filtered out of the book-lined room, oblivious of everything except their murmured conversations about ice cream and coffee houses. As the last of the pairs left, an aggressive silence invaded the room.

Tracing the silence to its source wasn't difficult. Clare sat comfortably ensconced in the chair she'd graced all evening. Soft lighting from a nearby brass floor lamp lent serenity to her face. Sam dropped into the worn leather chair behind his desk. He'd gone enough rounds in the corporate boardroom to recognize manipulation. If you wanted to keep the enemy on their toes, silence was an effective weapon. He'd used it himself. Nothing inspired self-doubt faster than a carefully orchestrated lull in the conversation.

Well, two could play the "quiet game." So Sam said nothing and peered at Clare over the stacks of files that littered his massive mahogany desk. Following his own advice, he took a good look at his partner. Proper southern belles never wore white before Easter, which explained Clare's pale pink linen suit. Lashes the same blue-black color of her hair fringed bottomless blue eyes, and small old-fashioned cameos decorated her ears. She wore her skirt short, which meant she knew she had great legs. Warming to his assignment, Sam moved on to other more delicious parts of her anatomy. He decided she probably made a conscious effort to hide the fullness of her breasts. Too bad.

"Like what you see?" inquired Clare. Only a touch of sarcasm seeped through her control.

Sam leaned back, propped his feet on his desk, and laced his hands behind his head. "Would it make a difference?" When she gave him a look designed to freeze the blood in his veins, he said, "Didn't think so. You'd rather be anywhere but here, wouldn't you?"

"I have more important things to do," Clare answered stiffly.

"Such as?" His tone implied serious doubt.

A slight huff escaped Clare, and she shifted in her chair. "What? You want a list?"

Sam nodded lazily. "I'm sure you've got one. Or two."

Suddenly Clare laughed. "Several. *You're* on one of them."

There it was again. That unexpected wit. Sam found himself liking Clare more every minute and damned if he could say why. Compulsively organized business executives weren't his style anymore. "Which list am I on?"

"Things I'm giving up for Lent."

"Giving things up for Lent," Sam repeated slowly, and thought for a moment. "Spent a lot of your life giving up things, Clare? Is that why you're so hell-bent on getting ahead?"

The question slammed into Clare like a fist. Was she so incredibly transparent? Or was Tucker simply taking the proverbial shot in the dark? If so, he had damned good night vision. But "giving up things" wasn't quite right. Giving up implied that she'd had something to begin with, and she hadn't really *had* anything since she was seven years old. Since her parents died and her aunt and uncle took her in and she became "poor little Clare."

Her aunt and uncle had things. Her cousin Ellie had whatever her heart desired. Clare McGuire had charity and was noticed only when she became tattered and faded. She could still hear her aunt. First the accusation as though she'd deliberately outgrown her clothes— *You've outgrown last year's dungarees!* And then the gentle rebuke—*For heaven's sake, why didn't you say something?*

"Clare. *Clare*," called Sam. "You're bruising my ego. That's the second time I've caught you daydreaming."

"What?" By degrees, Clare returned to the present, amazed at the vividness of her recollection, and at how easily a stray comment could bring back a forgotten moment. More than likely, Ellie's promised visit had prompted the childhood memories. Clare dredged up a smile. "Sorry. I already told you I have a lot on my mind. It's been a long week."

"It's only Tuesday."

"Yeah, well."

"Care to talk about it?"

"No!" Clare wanted to bite back the quick refusal and replace it with a gracious declination, but before she could, she realized her trip down memory lane had given Tucker the opportunity to drag his chair around the desk and angle it in front of hers.

Obviously Tucker seized opportunity as well as fun. He had one foot casually planted on either side of her chair, making it impossible for her to uncross her legs without asking him to move or tangling her legs with his. When Tucker leaned toward her expectantly, her focus narrowed to the rich tobacco brown of his eyes and the gentle concern mirrored there. Her breath escaped in a rush as she realized his concern was every bit as intimate as a kiss.

"Listen, Tucker," she blurted out. "I don't know what Dave told you—" She stopped, sighed, and shrugged. "Actually, I have a good idea what he told you. But I'm not obsessed. My secretaries aren't dropping like flies. I don't have problems, and I love my job."

Sam nodded wisely. "You're not like the others in the class. You shouldn't be here."

"Right." Relieved that he understood, she let out the breath she'd been holding. "I admit to having had five secretaries in three years, but not for the reasons Dave thinks. He thinks it's because I work too hard, demand too much. The truth is—you can't always get good help."

Dear God, she's serious, thought Sam. He studied his

hands and bit hard on the inside of his mouth before he said, "Maybe your expectations are too high."

"Hardly." Clare leaned toward him to make her point. "Well, maybe at first, but I've been worn down by a stream of well-meaning but undertrained assistants. Call me picky, but I like my paperwork filed according to the standard American alphabet. I like my telephone answered by the third ring. And *later dude* is not an acceptable closing phrase to any letter of mine!"

The laughter that had been building inside Sam got the better of him, and a chuckle escaped. Covering it quickly with a cough, he managed to push his amusement back long enough to say, "Sounds reasonable. You had no choice. You fired five secretaries."

"Not exactly," Clare mumbled.

"Excuse me?"

"Not exactly," she repeated more clearly, and settled back against the chair.

The way she retreated reminded Sam of an irritated feline, and the tiny rocking movements of her foot suggested the twitching of a cat's tail. She hadn't hissed or spat fire at him yet, but the night was still young. He could hope. And imagine. Anger would put sparks in her eyes and color in her cheeks. Passion would do that to her too, he decided. God, what a thought. *Those legs. Wrapped around him.*

Stunned, Sam jerked upright and pushed his chair backward across the hardwood floor. He wasn't exactly shaking, but was damn close to it. So he added another case of scotch to Dave's tab and reminded himself that he wasn't interested in obsessed company controllers who couldn't keep secretaries.

"Look, Tucker—" Clare began, mistaking his sudden

movement for impatience. "What does it matter how they left? They're gone."

She pushed a few wisps of hair away from her face with well-shaped fingernails, and Sam noticed the wedding ring for the first time. For a split second, overwhelming relief flooded through him. Married meant off limits. Then he felt disappointment and a slight stab of envy for her husband.

"Dave strikes again," he said softly, unaware that he'd spoken aloud.

"What does Dave have to do with this?" Puzzlement drew her brows together, and she tilted her head.

A breath of disgusted laughter slipped out of Sam as he rubbed the back of his neck. "Everything and nothing."

Clare studied him as he prowled around the room and wondered why he looked like a man wrestling with disappointment. Suddenly his words echoed in her mind—take a good look at your partner; decide if you like what you see. She wondered if he regretted the impulse that made them partners. With horror, she realized she cared about his answer.

And not just because his class was the key to her continued employment at Racing Specialties. His opinion mattered because he felt like one of *them*. One of the ones who always fit in, who always had friends, who never made mistakes. One of the ones who sealed your social fate with a welcoming grin or a disinterested nod.

Dear God, she breathed silently. For the first time in years, she suddenly felt like she'd been sized up, found wanting, and put outside the circle by one of *them*. Dammit all! It wasn't fair. She didn't want to feel like that again; she didn't want to care about other people's opinions. But she did. One class and the wall of indifference that kept her safe was beginning to crumble. And Tucker was to blame. Or Ellie. Or both of them. Or everything.

Uneasily Clare shook off the old demons and forced herself to concentrate. She had to ace this ridiculous course so she could keep her job long enough to hire secretary number six. With that thought in mind, she studied Tucker, looking for a key to his personality, something that she could use to her advantage. He was restless now. Like a man who wanted something he couldn't have.

Clare shifted, ran her tongue over dry lips, and recrossed her legs. Wondering why Tucker was restless made her nervous. Watching him pace played havoc with her whole nervous system. When he finally stopped beside a spiral staircase tucked unobtrusively in a corner, she whispered, "Thank God." Louder she asked, "Where does that lead?"

Absently Sam looked up. "Bedroom alcove."

"You *live* here?"

"No, but I sleep here occasionally."

"Why?"

When he hesitated, Clare stood up, dropped her day planner into the chair, and reminded him of the rules. "We're supposed to be finding out about each other. Over coffee. Since I don't drink coffee, we can skip that part of the assignment, but it should at least be my turn to ask the questions."

Sam considered that for a moment. "Okay. It's been a long time since I played truth or dare, but I'm game."

"Why do you sleep here?"

"Occasionally sleep here," Sam corrected her.

"Why do you *occasionally* sleep here?" Clare walked toward one book-lined wall.

Sam tried not to follow the gentle sway of her body as she wove a path between the chairs strewn about the room. "Sometimes I lose track of time, and the porch light goes off at midnight."

Intrigued, Clare turned and leaned against the high back of a Queen Anne chair. Sam's expression was bland as he met her gaze, no help at all in deciding if he was setting her up for a punch line. Whether he was or wasn't didn't matter. She had to ask. "Why do midnight and a porch light affect your sleeping arrangements?"

Shaking his head, Sam ignored her question and walked toward her. "My turn. What happened to your secretaries?"

"What is it with you and Dave and my secretaries?" Clare asked in frustration, digging her nails into the plush flame-stitched upholstery.

A wide old-fashioned windowsill made a good seat, so Sam plunked his rump down on it and stared pointedly at Clare. "You're the one who can't keep help. I'm just trying to find out why. If they didn't *exactly* get fired, then what *exactly* did happen?"

"They quit."

"I guessed that much. Why did they quit?"

She didn't answer immediately, and a blush began to stain her cheeks. Sam clasped his hands between his knees and called himself a fool. He had absolutely no business noticing how vulnerable she looked, because that made him want to hold her. And that was her husband's privilege, not his. His sense of timing where women were concerned was less than perfect.

"The general consensus is that I'm difficult to work for and have no sense of humor."

"That's what Dave thinks," Sam said gently. "And I can vouch for your sense of humor. So what do you think?"

"I think they didn't like me." Clare lifted her chin and waited for a reaction. She didn't expect a pleased smile, but that's what Sam gave her, a warm, approving, and slightly crooked smile.

"Good. That's the first honest thing you've said tonight." He hopped off the sill and stuck his hands in his back pockets. "Tell me something, Clare. Did these secretaries who didn't like you give *two* weeks notice?"

The question surprised her, and she tried to find the trick in it. She couldn't, so she answered. "They all gave two weeks notice."

"Then it wasn't you. People don't volunteer to work another two weeks for bosses they dislike. They'll work one because they need the good reference. But they won't work two. Maybe they left because they graduated McGuire boot camp and were ready for higher-paying jobs."

Clare's mouth dropped open in astonishment, but she snapped it shut quickly before she said something sappy like Do you really think so? Tucker already knew too many of her secrets without her volunteering any insecurities.

"Your turn," Sam said, and held his arms open, inviting her to take her best shot.

"I want to know about the porch light."

Sam rocked back and forth for a moment. "The porch light," he repeated. "You're from the South. You should know about porch lights."

"Born in New Orleans, but raised up north. I moved to Memphis only five years ago. Explain porch lights to me, Tucker."

"Explain porch lights," he repeated, and walked a few steps away. How did one explain southern tradition and old family retainers without sounding pretentious and hopelessly out of step with the modern world? As far as he could tell, his reputation was about to go right out the window.

"I live in the big house," he began.

Clare laughed and tucked her hair behind her ear. "The big house?"

Sam made a shushing sound and pointed to a chair. "Sit and listen. Yes, I live in the big house. I'm sure you noticed it when you drove around the corner—three stories, lots of ivy. Antiques, one helluva staircase and curving banister on the inside. The kind of house all good southern sons inherit from their fathers. It's a great house. The problem is that I also inherited the family butler, who turns off the porch light at midnight."

Pausing to make sure she was following him, Sam waited for her nod and then continued. "As far as he's concerned, a southern gentleman will either be home by twelve o'clock sharp or not at all. If I go through that door after midnight, William's liable to whack me on the head with a baseball bat and ask questions later."

While Sam slid into a nearby chair and swung a leg casually over the arm, Clare digested his explanation. Disbelief warred with amusement. "You can't go home after midnight because your own butler will attack you?"

"Well, not intentionally. He'd assume I was a burglar," Sam quickly added with a grin.

"Oh, well. *That* makes all the difference."

"I knew you'd understand. Now it's my turn. Where do you go for ice cream?"

Sam draped himself over a chair like a discarded quilt, his ease contagious. Clare leaned back and settled in, her crossed leg swinging gently and her hands folded on her thigh. "I don't go for ice cream."

"Ah." Sam nodded and touched his palm to his forehead. "I knew that. I'll bet you're the kind of woman who sends her husband for ice cream."

"What a great idea," Clare agreed enthusiastically. "Except I don't have a husband to send."

Every muscle in Sam's body tensed, and he realized he was angry with her. Angry because she didn't have a nice, safe husband. Angry because he liked her too much already. He didn't want to schedule his love life around production meetings and budget projections. He didn't want his breakfast table littered with spreadsheets and graphs. He didn't want to hear "Hold that thought while I make one more call." And he didn't want Dave snickering I-told-you-sos.

He knew exactly what dating Clare would be like, because he used to be the one with the schedule. He used to be the one snuffing out the romantic candles and turning on the light so he could read marketing proposals. While he was busy being busy, his girlfriend walked out and his father died.

When Clare's eyes widened, he knew some of his anger was showing in his facial expression. Sam undraped his leg and leaned his forearms on his thighs. He watched her closely as he said, "You wear a wedding ring."

Immediately she reached for the plain gold band and twisted the ring on her finger. "It was my mother's."

Sam had a grip on his emotions now, and the guilty

look in Clare's eye prompted him to say, "You wear it on your left hand."

"Doesn't fit my right."

"Isn't that handy!"

Freezing, Clare said, "Excuse me?"

"Isn't that handy," Sam repeated as he leaned back in his chair and studied her. "Most women would have had the ring sized or put it on a gold chain. But not you. You wear a wedding ring on your left hand and let people draw their own conclusions."

"What's your point, Tucker?" she asked softly.

"You use that ring to keep men at a distance." Sam pulled his chair up so that his thighs straddled her legs again. "I guess relationships are something else you don't have time for."

Seething, Clare flicked her eyes first at one long jean-clad thigh and then the other before raising her gaze to his face. She hated this feeling of exposure she got every time Sam invaded her space. She felt stripped naked and vulnerable beneath his patient gaze. Without warning, her pulse threatened to race out of control as she realized she wasn't seeing patience in his gaze.

She saw restrained hunger as he asked, "Is there any part of your life that you don't organize and control?"

"Ever had an impulse you *didn't* act on?" Clare shot back before she could stop herself.

His long, slow smile took her breath away. "Some of my favorite impulses are the ones I don't act on. Waiting is sometimes half the fun. Think about it. Anticipation and foreplay. One's mental. One's physical. Together they're mind-blowing."

Bells, whistles, and warning lights went off in Clare's head. *Foreplay.* Her heart slammed against her ribs and her chest constricted. Instinctively, she reached for her appointment-filled day planner as if to reassure herself that there was a real world outside the intimate circle the man in front of her had created with his body and provocative words.

Sensing her withdrawal, Sam twisted her own words and asked, "Ever had an impulse you *did* act on?"

Clare's chin came up. "Not that I'm particularly proud of."

"Well, at least you admit to having impulses."

"Are you done?" Clare asked, refusing the bait and eyeing the door. Without words she made her desire to leave very plain.

Sam scooted his chair back and watched her graceful exit. But when the door clicked softly behind her, he promised, "Lady, I'm just getting started."

TWO

"Last night? You want to know how last night went?" Clare asked, and leaned back in the no-nonsense executive chair that matched the functional furniture in her office.

Dave Gronski, owner and founder of Racing Specialties, grinned and shut the door. "Yeah. I'm your employer. I paid for the class. I'd like a report."

Feeling testy, Clare snapped, "I'll put it in a memo."

"Oooh!" Dave stretched out on her sofa, "Not so good, huh?"

"Why don't you ask your buddy?"

A chuckle rumbled across Dave's ample belly, which had been considerably larger thirty pounds ago. "How long did it take you to figure that out?"

"About three seconds. He called me Clare. *Before* we'd been introduced. Dammit, Dave. Did you have to give him a description? Didn't you trust me? I told you I'd show up for class."

"I didn't give him a physical description."

Clare tossed her mechanical pencil on a stack of com-

puter printouts and steepled her fingers. Dave appreci-
ated the value of plain speaking, and he was considerably
less volatile since his heart attack a few months back, but
Clare doubted his tolerance extended to being called a
liar. She contented herself with pressing her lips together
and looking at him out of the corner of her eye.

"Honest, Clare." Dave, mischief written all over his
face, tucked his thumbs behind his paisley suspenders. "I
didn't even tell him the color of your hair."

"Then how did he know me?"

"Lucky guess. Now, how did last night go?"

"Probably not as well as you wanted. Something
about me rubs that man the wrong way."

"No kidding," Dave murmured. Clare thought he
looked like the Cheshire cat would have looked if he'd
swallowed Alice's canary.

"I tried, Dave. Really. But every time I thought
things were going well, I'd say or do something that put
him on edge. For the life of me, I don't know what I
did." Casually, she picked up the pencil and rolled it
between her thumb and forefinger. "If things weren't
bad enough, I got stuck with him as my class partner."

Dave's eyebrows arched toward the ceiling. "Partner?"

"You heard me."

"And?"

"And we're supposed to research ice cream joints for
Saturday's field trip. Dave—" She propped her elbows
on the desktop. "Let's rethink this class idea. You know
that if I don't work Saturday, we won't be ready for the
new computers."

"I don't care if we're ready or not," Dave said
bluntly, and got up to leave. "I'll give you credit, Clare.

Five years ago you walked into my office and told me there wasn't a job you couldn't do. Well, you're the company controller now, and you can do every job around here, up to and including rebuilding a racing carburetor, but—"

"That's my point! It took a lot of hard work, but we are finally making some money around here. I don't want to blow it now. That's why it's so important for me to be *here* doing my—"

Dave cut her off. "Clare, no. You can do every job, but you can't do them all at once. Not twenty-four hours a day. I think one stress-induced heart attack per company is more than enough." Dave pulled open the door. "By the way, I like the new guy. Can we keep him?"

Clare hedged with a smile, "If he learns how to spell."

"Buy him a dictionary."

The big man wandered out of her office, having said what he came to say. He might sugar-coat his words with praise, but Clare understood the message. He had no intention of allowing her addiction to work to go any farther.

Alone again, she tried concentrating on the back-order printout. Initialing the report should have been a simple task, but she stared at the list for half an hour while Tucker's voice whispered to her, *People don't volunteer to work two weeks for bosses they dislike. One maybe because they need the reference, but not two.*

Clare pushed the intercom. "Joshua, come in here." As an afterthought, she pushed the button again. "Please."

❦ ———————— ❦

"William!" Sam bellowed, and hung over the second floor railing. There were times when he could positively choke his butler. Now was one of those times.

With great dignity the elderly man entered the marble-floored foyer below Sam and stopped. Before answering, he carefully adjusted a vase of flowers on a small table that dripped crocheted lace. To an innocent bystander, William might look like the perfect butler—starched white shirt, bow tie, pale parchment skin, hair peppered with gray, and a concerned facial expression that promised discretion.

But Sam knew better. Beneath that calm exterior lay one of the sharpest tongues on God's green earth. Forty years of employment with the Tucker family gave William the freedom to speak his mind, and he considered the Tucker children especially in need of guidance and wisdom. William didn't care that Sam was pushing thirty-three, or that his sister, Pamela, was closing in on thirty-five. William had known them since they were babies, and that was that. He might look like a butler, but he sounded more like a Dutch uncle.

"William—" Sam struggled to control his voice. "Have you seen my boxer shorts?"

"Why? Have you lost them?"

"No, I haven't lost them!"

"There is no call to raise your voice. I asked you a question, that's all. You leave those wild things all over the house as if you were raised in a barn."

Sam ground his teeth. He was well aware of William's opinion of his boxer collection. The gospel according to William said that gentlemen came home before midnight and wore white underwear instead of wild prints and neon polka dots. "William, what have you *done* to my boxer shorts?"

Folding his hands behind him, the butler considered the question for a moment. "Done?"

Exasperated, Sam waved a pair of shorts decorated with billiard balls. "Someone has sewn name tags in every pair of boxers I own. I haven't had name tags in my underwear since I went to summer camp twenty years ago!"

"Ah," William ackowledged as though light dawned in his memory. "I had Rebecca do that. I was worried about you losing them, seeing as how you can't find the clothes hamper."

Sam silently counted to ten before he said anything, and then realized that while he was dressed in a bath towel, nothing he could say would sound the least bit dignified. Disgusted, he snapped the shorts against the railing and walked away. When he entered the master bedroom, he grimaced. Yesterday's clothes still lay where he'd dropped them—first when he'd changed for class and then again when he'd stripped for bed.

The floor of his room might as well have been a chess game played with cast-off clothing. Crumpled socks represented pawns. Cowboy boots and tennis shoes became castles. Blue jeans were knights, and boxers in paisley and plaid were well-guarded kings.

He stared at the clothes, realizing what a difference a couple of years could make. Two years earlier his father had still been alive—grieving over the loss of his wife, but alive. Two years earlier Sam's clothes had hung neatly in closets or been carefully tucked away in drawers. He'd used a custom-made valet for his cuff links and ties. His priorities had been different then too, Sam reminded himself as he dressed quickly. Back then he'd wanted a trophy wife, top-of-the-line golf clubs, and an expensive house on the eighteenth hole.

After his father's death he'd spent a year and a half in a guilt-driven depression before his sister finally made him see that he couldn't change the past. He could, however, change the future. So he'd found a buyer for his export company—a buyer who also paid him a healthy consulting fee each year.

Changing the habits of a lifetime had taken another six months, but in doing so he discovered what he wanted out of life. He wanted family—kids, a big dog, and someone comfortable to wake up with. He wanted holidays and fights over the Sunday paper. He was thirty-three years old and ready to settle down.

Which was why he had no business falling in lust with one of his work-obsessed students.

Sam grabbed the boots from the floor and cursed his luck and Clare McGuire. They amounted to the same thing. Clare wasn't the type to fight over the Sunday funnies. Probably didn't read the comics. Probably didn't even talk at the breakfast table. Everything about her was wrong for a man looking for a family.

Then why does she get to you?

"Hell if I know," Sam answered himself, and strode purposefully out of the house. The large oval of etched glass rattled in the front door as he slammed it behind him.

Sam didn't feel the smallest twinge of guilt, but he was certain the game of hide-and-seek Clare had been playing was about to end. For three days he had tried to get her on the phone. If he called her at home, the machine answered. If he called her at work, her male secretary, Joshua, answered, made an excuse, and took a message that went straight into the garbage can. However, today's message couldn't be crumpled and tossed.

This message was going to be delivered in person. Sam stood in front of Joshua's desk and looked him squarely in the eye.

Joshua put down the phone and collected himself. Sam decided Clare's secretary looked like a Joshua. He had a boyish innocence, but he couldn't tell a good lie to save his life. Even several days of practice hadn't improved his technique.

"I'm sorry, sir. Miss McGuire won't be able to see you. She has a . . . prior appointment," the young man advised as he settled his wire-rimmed glasses more firmly on his face. Only the slight waiver in his voice exposed his nervousness.

"What appointment?" Sam asked, deciding that Clare's vague excuses needed to be tested.

"What appointment?" Joshua's words were almost a squeak.

"Yes. Is she meeting someone? Is someone coming here? Can I wait until she's free? Is she sneaking out to play on a beautiful Friday afternoon? Or did she just tell you to get rid of me?" Sam tilted his head in a silent demand for an answer.

Guilt showed plainly on Joshua's face as his eyes slid toward Clare's closed office door. "Look, Mr. Tucker, I don't know what the two of you are fighting about. Hell, I didn't even know she had a boyfriend. I'm sorry, but she told me to hold your calls all week. Today she even swore. She never does that. Then she said she should have known you couldn't take a hint and told me to get rid of you again." Joshua dropped his voice. "I think she's afraid to see you."

Afraid to see him? Why would she be afraid? Unless . . . unless he got to her the same way she got to him. A sudden surge of anticipation thumped against Sam's rib cage at the possibility. He felt a smile of satisfaction tug at the corners of his mouth.

"I see," he said quietly.

Relief flooded Joshua's features, and he pushed up his glasses again. "Man, am I glad you understand. I'm new. I took this temporary job because I can't afford college, and I love everything about engines. I got an A in typing class, but"—Joshua leaned toward him—"I don't have a clue about office politics and this administrative stuff."

"Oh, getting ahead in the corporate environment is easy. There's only one rule—never, *ever* tell the truth to anyone. Unless your boss tells you to." As Sam spoke, he moved toward Clare's office. Joshua realized his intention and reached for the intercom buzzer just as Sam jerked open the door and leaned against the jamb. "Hello, Clare. Is your answering machine at home broken? Or are you just ignoring me?"

Conflicting emotions flooded Clare as she stared at the man who casually filled her doorway as though he belonged in her life. Anger wrestled with inexplicable pleasure and enjoyment as she took a physical inventory of Tucker, unable to find fault with the lean, well-muscled man in front of her. She knew the sting in her cheeks was a guilty blush, and that tipped the scales toward anger. She wasn't wrong. He was. What right did he have invading her privacy?

Then she remembered how he'd invaded her space

before, one leg on either side of hers, leaning forward, ignoring every unwritten rule of social conduct. Tucker wasn't the kind of man who waited for an invitation. And he obviously wasn't the kind of man who could be ignored.

"My phone works perfectly," Clare said, shaking her head at Joshua, who offered to call security. Her secretary backed away, looking decidedly relieved, and Clare's gaze returned to her uninvited guest. "What do you want, Tucker?"

"That's a question you should be asking yourself. Maybe I'm confused, but I thought your job depended on taking my class seriously." He shouldered away from the frame and kicked the door shut with his heel. "I thought partners worked together."

"My job depends on how well I do it," Clare corrected him. "And we're partners in this ridiculous assignment only because you tricked me."

Sam gave a short, humorless laugh and crossed the room in three lazy strides that swirled tension into the air. When he stopped in front of her desk, he put his hands on the edge and leaned forward. "Your job depends on how well Dave thinks you do it. And we're partners because you didn't pay any more attention in class than you have to my phone calls."

When her eyes widened nervously, Sam straightened, backing away. He hadn't intended to frighten her. Hell, he hadn't done anything *to* frighten her, but she acted as if he'd crossed some invisible barrier.

Slowly, he sank into a chair and considered what he knew of Clare. He remembered her silence when asked if she'd had a lot of practice giving things up. He recalled the look of instant panic in the carriage house when he'd pulled his chair in front of her and slid his legs on either side of hers. He remembered a husbandless wedding ring. Why was keeping people at a distance so important to her?

"Poor Clare," he whispered, unknowingly using the one phrase that could twist a knife in her heart. "I scare you because I don't respect your flawless efficiency or the invisible wall that keeps people out." His eyes caught and held hers. "I expect the real Clare to come out and play. And that scares the hell out of you."

Clare wanted to call him a liar. She wanted him to leave. She wanted to forget his class. Unfortunately, what she wanted didn't seem to matter anymore, and the most she could manage was a weak "That's absurd."

"Is it?" The question hung in the air.

"Of course it is."

"Then come out and play."

Quiet engulfed the room as Clare realized he wasn't talking about class assignments and research. Warmth exploded in the pit of her stomach, and blood rushed to her cheeks. *Come out and play?* She'd sooner play with matches in a dynamite factory.

Sitting across from a man who turned her inside out was a new experience for Clare, and she didn't much like it. Didn't like constantly fighting her body's reckless re-action to the invitation in his smiles. Didn't like the way she forgot how to breathe every time he leaned toward her. Or admitting, even to herself, that she had looked at every inch of his long, hard body as he stood in the doorway. For a brief moment she'd even wondered how she would feel cradled between his thighs, her belly rocked against—

Panic filled her soul again and she bit off the

thoughts. The blush rose higher in her cheeks, and without looking she knew that her turquoise silk blouse did little to hide the awakening peaks of her breasts. *Why now?* she thought. *Why him?* And then the most frightening thought of all as she looked into warm brown eyes that promised laughter: *Why not him?*

"Clare! I want to talk to you." Dave's voice boomed from outside the door a second before he threw it open. He clutched a pink telephone message like a shield, and he waved it at her.

"Hello, Dave," Sam interrupted. "Ever considered knocking?"

"Why should he?" Clare asked, and folded her arms across her chest. "You don't."

Dave turned his head from side to side, as though making a silent judgment about the scene in front of him. His eyes narrowed, and he looked at Sam. "This is a message from you. Why do you need to talk to me about Clare?"

Clare was on her feet instantly, hands on her hips. "You called Dave? Why, of all the rotten—"

Sam struggled for an explanation. He'd called Dave after slamming down the phone on another of Joshua's lame excuses. At the time, he'd intended to toss Clare out of his class. Now he wasn't so sure he wanted to do that. Not yet.

"Well, Sam?" Dave asked again.

Two pairs of eyes glared at him, demanding an explanation, but Sam didn't spare the big man a glance. His attention was riveted on the woman across from him. Clare was mad as hell. Anger had replaced the vulnerability in her eyes, and Sam discovered that her anger put them on equal footing again.

"Settle an argument for me, Dave," Sam said softly without turning his head. "Is Clare's job in jeopardy?"

Clare's blue eyes widened, and the sparks of anger abruptly winked out only to reappear. "Don't answer that, Dave!"

"I think you need to hear the answer. *Really* hear it, because I wouldn't fire you." Dave paused dramatically and crumpled the telephone message. "But I would suspend you for six weeks and pull an audit of your entire department."

Clare's legs felt suddenly weak, and she put a hand on the desk to steady herself. "You wouldn't."

"Would and will," Dave answered curtly. "Constant stress leads to more than heart attacks; it leads to mistakes. Costly mistakes. So I suggest you start cooperating with Sam and get rid of some of that stress you pretend isn't there. Now, why are you here, Sam?"

"Social call. I'm taking your controller out for dinner and ice cream."

"Excuse me!" Clare said, and narrowed her eyes. "I don't remember agreeing to go to the elevator with you. Much less to dinner."

Sam laughed when Dave raised an eyebrow. "We're still negotiating."

"Need an arbitrator?" he offered.

"All right. That's it," Clare warned ominously. "I've had it with you two. You might control my professional life at the moment, and you can force me to take this stupid class. But you do not control whom I go out with."

"Why? You already have a better offer for tonight?" Sam asked.

"No, I don't have a—" Clare stopped, realizing that

she'd just blown the one excuse that would have wiped the smug look of triumph off Tucker's face.

"Good-bye, Dave," Sam said smoothly, moving to open the door for his friend. "I think I can handle it from here."

Clare sourly noted that her boss had the decency not to laugh until Tucker closed the door behind him. Hearing his guffaws forced her to take several deep breaths to calm her temper. God, what a situation. Tucker wouldn't stop until she let go of the comfortable routine that kept her safe, that structured her life. But if she said no, she risked her job. Dave was a born-again workaholic out to save the world from his mistakes. He was serious about her participation in the burnout program.

Tucker stood silently by the door. Waiting to pounce, Clare decided. She approached him slowly and stopped a foot away. Defeat echoed in her voice as she spoke. "What do you want from me?"

"I want you to come out and play. With me. Is that so awful?"

"Not awful," Clare whispered, suddenly aware of him as a man as well as the enemy. "Dangerous. I like my life the way it is, and you want to change me."

The vulnerability was back in her gaze, and Sam felt the familiar tightening in his belly, the need to pull her close and promise her anything that would erase the uncertainty in her eyes. At the same time, he recognized a desire that had nothing to do with comforting. Her lips were slightly parted, and when her tongue brushed moisture on them, he knew she was right. The game he played was dangerous. He wanted more than her honest participation in his class.

He leaned toward her slowly, giving her the opportunity to pull back. She didn't. His hands found the rounded curves of her shoulders, and he let himself enjoy the feel of silk-covered flesh beneath his fingers. His hands moved to cup her neck, and his head dipped lower. Her bottom lip was full, and it fascinated him. He wanted to—

Abruptly, he jerked himself back from making the mistake of kissing her. What he *wanted* and what she needed were two different things. She needed to trust him first. Which meant she had to spend time with him.

"So—" The word was little more than a rasp. He cleared his throat and tried again. "So, what time should I pick you up?"

Clare blinked and sucked in an uneven breath against the disappointment that coursed through her. Knowing she'd wanted his kiss began the burning panic in her stomach again. How could she want to kiss a man whose only interest was in changing her? How was that possible? Obviously her libido had little use for logic.

And now he expected her to go to dinner with him? Be alone with him for hours? That was madness. Or torture. Or both. *Do you have a choice?*

"What if I say I can't go tonight?"

"What if you tell me why?" Sam countered. "And don't tell me you're washing your hair. That couldn't take more than five minutes."

Clare raised a self-conscious hand to her hair and flicked it away from her face. She kept it short to save time, but suddenly she wondered if it was too short.

"I like short hair," Sam said with a smile as if he could read her thoughts.

"So do I," Clare said, and looked pointedly at his long mane of wheat and gold.

"I like short hair on women," Sam amended. "What time should I pick you up?"

"I need to clean house. Ellie's coming and—" Clare knew how utterly ridiculous that sounded, given her circumstances. "You don't care, do you?"

Sam shook his head. "What time should I pick you up?"

"Five-thirty, but I need to be home early."

"Why?" Sam asked as he pulled open the door. "Tomorrow's Saturday."

Because I'm afraid to spend any more time with you than absolutely necessary.

"Look, Sam. I agreed to go. I'm trying. Isn't that enough?"

"It's a start, Clare. It's a start."

Clare frantically searched the mound of clothes in the armchair for a clean pair of jeans. Slick, her cat, yowled at her as she disturbed him and dumped him unceremoniously onto the floor. She had to have a pair of jeans in the mountainous pile of unfolded laundry. She *had* to. Relief flooded through her as she unearthed faded blue denim. Experience told her a couple of turns in the dryer would smooth out the wrinkles.

"This is why everything should go to the cleaners," Clare informed the huge cat who was half Maine coon cat and half mystery cat. He blinked his eyes, twitched his tail, and hissed once, still clearly miffed about losing his bed of clothes.

"Keep that up, and I'll have you neutered," Clare threatened as she passed him.

While the jeans tumbled in the dryer, Clare took a shower and put on fresh makeup. Slick sat on the side of the basin, an appraising look in the yellow slits of his eyes as he watched her preparations. His tail lashed an irritating, reproachful rhythm. Finally, Clare slammed her eye makeup compact into the medicine cabinet and glared at him. "Well, thank you for your support. If I had a choice, do you think I'd be going?"

Clare thought about that as she pulled her jeans from the dryer and slid her legs into the warm cotton fabric. The copper zipper was hot against her stomach as she gave a little hop and smoothed the jeans over her hips. Slowly, she zipped them and buttoned the waist.

What would she have said if Sam's invitation had been personal instead of motivated by his responsibility as her class partner? *He almost kissed you and you don't think his invitation was personal?* An almost-kiss didn't mean anything to men like Sam, Clare told herself.

Tucker had a loose, easy charm that meant absolutely nothing. Nothing, she cautioned herself. He was out to prove his point—that he could change her. She was a challenge to him. Sort of a test for his class. And if she were smart, she'd remember that. She'd forget the unfamiliar feelings that swamped her when he looked at her. She'd concentrate on giving him what he wanted without letting him touch the real Clare.

She was good at pretending to be what people wanted. She'd done it all her life. Playing Tucker's game was simply another bit of make-believe. She'd go out. She'd have a good time. She'd say and do all the right things. And then she'd forget Tucker until the next assignment.

That's how she'd handle him, one assignment at a time. In six weeks he'd be gone. Slipping on just one dangling enamel earring, Clare smiled slowly at her reflection and went to answer the doorbell.

THREE

As Sam rang Clare's doorbell for the second time, the painted, deep-green door opened as wide as the security chain permitted. One half of her face appeared in the opening, and she startled Sam with a welcoming smile that he would have sworn conveyed genuine pleasure at his arrival. Uncertainly, he leaned back and eyed the black metal numbers on the side of the condominium.

"You're in the right place, Tucker," Clare said.

"I wasn't sure for a moment," he said bluntly. A smile escaped him as his attention was suddenly claimed by a very large, tawny-tipped gray paw that reached tentatively through the opening to catch the edge of his trousers. Sam decided the feline gesture was an invitation. "May I come in?"

"No." The answer was immediate and punctuated by the door's closing.

Sam's mouth dropped open at the speed with which her face and the paw had disappeared from view. Left alone on her doorstep, he wondered at the abrupt change in her welcoming attitude. From behind the door he heard the chain rattle and what sounded like a muffled "Shut up, Slick." A few moments later Clare slithered out the door.

Slither *was* the correct word. She opened the door a crack and skimmed through without revealing any of the room behind her. Sam realized Slick was the cause of her exaggerated movements, and grinned. Punctual, precise Clare McGuire slithered out of her house because she lived with an escape-artist cat.

"Well, I'm ready," Clare announced breathlessly as she whirled away from locking the door.

Her hair flared and danced around her ears before settling into the familiar, shiny blue-black cap. An earring Sam could describe only as flirty dangled from one ear. The other lobe was conspicuously bare, and so was one shoulder. Or at least covered by so little, it might as well have been bare. She wore an off-the-shoulder, abbreviated University of Memphis jersey that exposed a quarter-inch of creamy midriff as she slung a small purse over her shoulder. While he stared, Sam said a silent thank-you for an unseasonably warm spring.

Unexpectedly, awareness prickled the back of his neck as he became cognizant that he wasn't the only one staring! Clare's gaze roamed as freely as his, and not for the first time. She'd looked at him this way before, when he leaned against the door frame of her office. He felt his muscles tense. Objectively, he understood that what was sauce for the goose was sauce for the gander, but this was different. The woman's gaze had actually run the length of him, stopping briefly at his hips.

Oh, and your inspection was purely platonic? his conscience asked. Silencing his morally upright conscience,

Sam pointed toward the parking lot and tried to figure out why Clare's frank appraisal jangled his calm.

Clare followed the familiar winding walkway toward the parking area, glad to be moving, glad to have an excuse to look away from Sam and concentrate on the white-blossomed dogwoods along the walkway. She had felt devoured beneath his scrutiny, but she would have bitten her tongue before she'd said a word. Instead, she returned the favor, and judging from his reaction, she'd finally managed to rattle him. Of course, her choice of clothing might have had something to do with his reaction. He'd been expecting prim-and-proper Clare, not the Gypsy who'd answered her door.

And she'd expected him to arrive in clothes selected at random more for their comfort than appropriateness. Instead, he wore pinpoint oxford in pale pink, and khaki pants obviously tailored by an expert. Briefly, she felt flattered, but instantly crushed the emotion. Tucker wasn't trying to impress her. More likely he was trying to soften her up so he could slip past her guard. Not likely, she promised herself.

"Which one?" Clare asked as she balanced on the curb and surveyed the numerous cars in the lot.

"The black one." Sam pointed and placed a gentle hand on her back to urge her forward.

Clare rebelled at the intimacy of such a casual gesture. His touch wasn't lecherous. That she could have disliked and dismissed. No, Tucker touched because . . . because, she suspected, he didn't know how to be any other way. That he had no idea of the havoc he engendered in her each time he touched her forced her to deal with the fact that she liked his touch.

Suddenly Clare realized she hadn't moved an inch

and that Tucker's hand still rested against the small of her back, skin touching skin in the brief space between waistband and shirt edge. Clare took an unsteady step toward the car he indicated and then stopped short, turning to gape at him. A second look at the car brought a peal of laughter.

"A Volvo?" Her voice shook with amusement. "Live-for-the-moment devil-may-care Sam Tucker drives a *Volvo*? The safest car made?" She grabbed the door handle and wrenched open the door. "Jeez! And you think *I* have no sense of adventure?"

Sam leaned across the top of the car to defend his transportation, but she disappeared into the automobile with an unladylike snort that eloquently expressed her opinion. The car rocked as Sam dropped behind the wheel. He wanted to argue with her, to dispute the stodgy image of a Volvo, but he couldn't. She was right. The car was a remnant of his practical past.

"Okay. I don't have a sports car." Sam started the engine. "But that's the point I'm trying to make with this class. You don't have to overhaul your entire life. All you have to do is make a few changes."

Locking her seat belt, Clare let an exasperated sigh slip out. "Tucker, you are like a dog with a bone! Why don't you take a page out of your own book and make a few changes yourself. You're the one who's so tradition bound, you can't fire your baseball-toting butler!"

"I wasn't aware you could fire family," Sam said flatly.

"Butlers aren't family."

"I wouldn't say that in front of William if I were you."

"You're serious!" Clare exclaimed, and found the idea oddly satisfying. "About him being family, I mean."

"Dead serious. A mere servant couldn't be nearly as irritating as William can be. And why can't William be family? Have you got rules about family too?"

"No rules. Just experience."

Sam looked quickly over at Clare's blank expression and then returned his attention to merging into the kamikaze traffic on the torn-up I-240 expressway loop. Threading his way through the confusion of highway construction reminded him of how carefully he had to negotiate the secrets of Clare's past.

"Experience?" he echoed. "Exactly what *is* family in your experience?"

Outside the car, orange drums and concrete sped past as Clare chewed on her bottom lip. What was family? She didn't know. She could tell him what family *wasn't*. But not what family was. Her aunt dutifully called every Christmas and extended the holiday invitation. Clare always managed a plausible excuse and was rewarded with her aunt's tiny sigh of relief. Each year Christmas cheer was delivered by men in brown uniforms driving brown trucks.

Without looking away from the window, Clare said, "I'm an orphan."

Immediately, the car slowed as Sam physically felt the impact of her words. Just as quickly, though, he recovered, and the Volvo resumed speed. "Sorry. Didn't mean to pry."

"Don't be sorry," Clare ordered. "I told you. I didn't have to. And don't *feel* sorry for me either. I had good food, clean clothes, and a roof over my head."

"But that wasn't enough, was it?" Sam asked quietly, and this time he was prying.

No! It wasn't enough. I wanted to be first just once when Uncle Pat came home from a trip. I wanted to be the first one swooped up and tossed into the air. I wanted to hear Uncle Pat say, "I missed my girl!" And, damn you, Tucker, I want you to stop pushing the buttons.

But Clare didn't say any of that. Instead, she plastered a smile on her face and lied. "I did all right. And contrary to what you might think. I'm even happy."

"Except about my class," Sam goaded, and steered the car onto the off ramp and the conversation into safer waters.

"I am especially unhappy about your class."

Before she could elaborate, her attention was captured by the neighborhood, its familiarity nagging at her. Enormous oak trees draped over the streets, forming a natural arbor. Wrought iron railings marched around the perimeter of yards that belonged in garden magazine layouts. In this area of town, hundred-year-old homes were the rule, not the exception. And despite all its upscale touches, the neighborhood possessed character not found in modern subdivisions. The houses had architectural quirks, and oddities unique to this particular section of Memphis.

Uneasily she realized it was familiar because she'd driven down streets just like this one on her way to Tucker's class. Four blocks later, she stopped fighting her suspicions. Ice encased her words as she asked, "Tucker, where the hell do you think you're going?"

"Midtown."

"Yes, thank you. I can see that. I drove down this street last Tuesday."

"Then you know my house isn't much farther."

Clare adjusted the shoulder on her jersey. "I guess you've cleverly planned an intimate little dinner?"

Without bothering to flip on his blinker, Sam turned the corner and grinned at her. "Well, that's what *I* planned, but as far as William's concerned, I'm bringing you home to meet the family. Which means he'll be annoyingly underfoot all evening." The Volvo slid to a stop in front of the big house. "Ready?"

"No." Confused, Clare asked, "If William's going to ruin all your devious plans, why did you bring me here?"

"*Because* William will ruin all my devious plans. With him around, maybe you'll relax and enjoy yourself." Sam opened his door. "Besides, no one in town makes a better bacon, lettuce, and tomato sandwich. Come on. William's hovering in the foyer, waiting to greet us and pretending to be my butler."

Clare got out of the car and tried to figure out how to handle the situation. On the one hand, she knew an intimate little dinner with Sam would be a self-control accident waiting to happen. But she couldn't quite wish away the tiny feeling of disappointment that sank into her bones when she found out that she wasn't going to be in a candlelit room, swirling wine in a crystal glass, and wondering when he'd kiss her. And then she realized she hadn't once thought about the office in the last half hour.

As she approached the door, Clare decided that this was a house for romance. The glow of polished walnut and brass framed an oval panel of frosted glass etched with flowering vines. Silently the door opened, and an elderly man bowed, or, rather, bent stiffly at the waist for a fraction of a second.

"Evenin', Miss Clare."

"I hate it when he does his proper-southern-butler routine," Sam muttered to Clare as he put a hand on the small of her back and urged her across the threshold. "Good evening, William." Sam did a quick double take as he passed the man. "White gloves?"

William's smile evaporated into a thin line of disapproval as he shut the door. "And what's wrong with a little respect for the lady? It's been long enough since we've seen one in this house. My memory isn't so good anymore, but I remember how to treat a lady, even if you don't."

"What's that supposed to mean?" Sam demanded, and scowled at Clare when a strangled sound—suspiciously like a laugh—escaped her.

"I mean, in my day we took a lady out properly. Bought her dinner in a nice restaurant."

"But this isn't a date," Clare said quickly. Too quickly. And she knew it. Both men looked at her, tilted their heads and raised their eyebrows in that infuriatingly male way that silently suggested she was confused. "No, it's true, William. I'm here only because Sam blackmailed me."

That wiped the smug look off Sam's face. Satisifed, Clare continued. "He said if I didn't go out with him, I'd miss the world's best BLT sandwich." Clare gave William a half-smile.

"Hmmph. He ought to know. The boy's eaten enough of 'em over the years."

"Do you use thick-sliced country bacon?" Clare asked hopefully.

William put his hands on his hips and demanded, "Now, what else would I use?"

"I'll bet you cut the strips in half and layer them

between thin, ripe tomato slices." When he nodded, Clare added, "If you tell me you lightly toast the bread, I can die a happy woman."

In disbelief, Sam watched Clare finesse his butler with the skill of a tournament bridge player. William straightened as he realized that here was a woman who would appreciate his talents. Just the right amount of flattery mixed with a basic human need like hunger sent William scurrying off to do her bidding.

"Been handling servants long?" Sam asked as William's back disappeared.

"All my life."

"You're an orphan."

"Yeah, I remember." Clare dropped her purse on the foyer table.

"Poor little rich girl?" Sam asked.

"No." The jersey slid off her shoulder again.

Clear blue eyes stared into his, unwavering and unfathomable. She didn't tug her shirt up or offer any more explanations—her tactful way of telling Sam that the subject was closed. Sam got the message, but wondered why her secrets had the power to twist tiny knots in his gut. Unraveling her past was becoming important to him. Important enough that he couldn't let the sight of a creamy-white shoulder make him forget the dangers of being more than a friend to a woman like her.

Breaking the uncomfortable silence, Clare motioned toward the interior of the house. "Who else lives here?"

"Just me. And William. Come on. I'll give you the nickel tour. That's about all it's worth unless you like antiques."

"Love 'em," Clare admitted. "But I figured you for

glass and chrome. Recessed lighting. Linear paintings in obnoxious colors."

Sam smoothed a hand along the massive banister as he escorted Clare past the stairs. "You like putting people into neat little boxes crammed with your expectations of them, don't you, Clare?"

"I didn't mean—"

"Yes, you did," Sam said gently. "But to answer you, I haven't changed a stick of furniture since my parents died. The family joke was that Mama had no taste. The woman wore plaid with polka dots and went out in public. Dad said when he bought her this house, she went down to Antiques-R-Us and bought the deluxe twenty-one-room package. But the truth was, she loved this house. She chose every piece of furniture, every pillow."

His obvious affection for his mother tugged at Clare's heart. She knew what losing a parent felt like, but she didn't have the memories. She couldn't reach into her mind and pull out a hundred funny and touching stories. She couldn't play "remember when." Not the way Ellie could, and sometimes she hated Ellie because of it. And she hated herself for feeling jealous over something that was never Ellie's fault.

Shaking off the black thoughts, Clare followed Sam through rooms filled with curios and cabinets. His mother's style had been more eclectic than disciplined, but the effect was warm and timeless. Clare itched to kick off her shoes and dig her toes in the thick, patterned rugs that hugged hardwood floors—something she'd never wanted to do in her aunt's house. Something she hadn't been allowed to do in her aunt's house.

By the time they finished the tour, William had dinner on the table in the "family" dining room. The room had a Shakerlike quality of simplicity, as if it had been designed to minimize distraction during meals. A massive oak trestle table was flanked by two padded benches instead of chairs.

"Exactly how many brothers and sisters do you have?" Clare asked when she realized the table could easily seat twelve people.

"One sister, but Mama always wanted a brood. That's why she bought the table. She never got the large family, but by then she'd grown attached to the table."

Clare laughed. "Or your father couldn't face the thought of having to move the thing!"

The swinging door from the kitchen opened, and William brought in their meal. "If you're through draggin' Miss Clare all 'round this old house, you might let her sit down and eat this food."

"Careful, Clare," Sam warned as he sat down across from her. "I think William likes you. If you don't watch it, he'll start trying to run your life too."

"Hmmph," William huffed as he banged the iced tea glasses down on the table. He left the room, but not before firing a well-aimed parting shot. "Some folks could do with a little advice. If you'd listened to me, you wouldn't have been alone for the last two years. By the way, Rebecca said she could take the name tags out of your boxer shorts anytime you're ready."

Clare was torn between two strong emotions—rampant curiosity and laughter. The stunned expression on Sam's face forced the laughter. With a few choice words William had managed to do something Clare had been trying to do since she met Sam—whittle him down to size.

"God, I hate my butler." Sam's pained and humorless

laugh joined hers. "I can't fire him, but I may have to kill him."

Laughter subsided into tiny sighs that sounded suspiciously like chuckles. Sobering, Clare pulled her napkin from beneath her silverware and opened her mouth to ask the question that had to be asked.

"Don't ask," Sam ordered, knowing she'd ignore him anyway.

"Aren't you a little old to have name tags in your underwear?"

"What do you think?" Sam asked, and bit off a corner of his sandwich.

Clare's mouth hurt from the effort of keeping a grin off her face. "Then why do you have name tags in your underwear?"

Sam contemplated slow tortures for William. How could he explain about the name tags without revealing his status as a world-class slob? A woman as compulsively organized as Clare would certainly get a hoot out of that story. No, he'd rather not tell it. "It's a long story."

"Okay," agreed Clare as she speared a green bean. "You don't have to talk about your boxers. We can talk about why you've been alone for the last two years."

"No, we can't. And don't believe everything William says."

"Do you have name tags in your underwear?"

Sam dropped his half-eaten sandwich to his plate and shoved it away. "Yes, I do, but that's beside the point."

"Have you brought a woman home in the last two years?"

"What difference does it make?"

"I don't know." Clare sipped her tea and smiled into

the bottom of the glass before she looked up. "But I'm having fun. Isn't that what you wanted?"

The topic of conversation was not one he would have chosen, but Sam had to admit that Clare was definitely relaxed. She hadn't mentioned the office, or cleaning her house, or the long list of unfinished tasks waiting for her. She seemed perfectly content to enjoy William's culinary masterpiece and quiz him about his underwear and his love life. If he hadn't known better, he'd have accused Clare of flirting. "Why this sudden interest in me?"

"Turnabout's fair play. It's been open season on my life history from the moment I met you. Now it's my turn. I'm getting to know my partner. Remember?"

"All right," Sam agreed, and wondered if Clare realized that by admitting her curiosity, she'd taken a step toward seeing him as a person and not the enemy. "What do you want to know?"

"Why haven't you brought a woman home in the last two years?"

Sam drew his thumb down the side of his tea glass, wiping away the moisture that clung to it. "I was busy having a midlife crisis."

"Aren't you a little young for a midlife crisis?"

"Trust me. When your father dies, you instantly become middle-aged. Regardless of how young you are." Sam heard the bitterness in his voice and wished her question hadn't struck that particular nerve.

Once again Clare felt a flash of empathy for Sam. As he stared into his glass, his eyes looked old. Almost dead. Clare wondered if that's how other people saw her, and knew she didn't like the comparison. Sam dragged his gaze back to hers, and the spark in his eyes ignited. Sam was Sam again.

"So I did what any self-respecting man would do. I changed my entire life. Sold my business, sold my condo at Southwind, and burned my day planner."

Choking on her tea, Clare covered her mouth with her hand and snatched her napkin out of Sam's hand as he held it toward her. "Day planner? *You* had a day planner? I thought you couldn't plan fun."

"I didn't. I planned my life. Right down to the second. I planned for everything. Except I didn't plan to lose the lady in my life." Sam stood up abruptly and fought the urge to blurt out that he hadn't planned on being so busy that his father, already devastated by his wife's death, killed himself from loneliness. The guilt of not making time for his father was suddenly very near the surface, and he knew this wasn't the time or place to talk about the skeletons rattling in his conscience.

"Come on," Sam said, and motioned toward the front of the house. "Let's get out of here and find some ice cream. I'll tell you all about my blighted love life and how just mentioning William scares most women away."

Clare popped the last bite in her mouth and took a swig of tea. "Shouldn't we tell William we're going?"

Taking her elbow and guiding her away from the kitchen door, Sam said, "No need. I'm sure he heard everything we said."

Beyond the door, a metal pot clanged loudly into a counter, and Clare heard a disgruntled "Hmmph."

"Well, what'll it be?"

Clare looked around and decided Sam had a screw loose if he thought she was going to eat anything prepared inside the shack in front of her. Yellow lights beneath the awnings glowed in the twilight, and the menu was a bulletin board crowded with a patchwork of faded paper. Prices had been written on the paper, scratched through, and written again. Bright neon starbursts were tacked on every available surface, and bold Magic-Marker printing promised new taste sensations like Passion Sundaes and Raspberry Fudge Rhapsody.

Overwhelmed, Clare simply stared at the large concrete drainage ditch that flanked the ice cream joint. People seated in the al fresco area of cinder-block benches were oblivious of their surroundings, unbothered by the exhaust fumes from the busy intersection that invaded the air. The redneck honky-tonk across the street began to rock and roll as four-wheel-drive truck doors slammed in a predictable rhythm.

"You gotta be kidding me," she finally said.

"I never joke about ice cream."

Clare lowered her voice. "Sam, do you see a posted health certificate? I don't."

"Inside on the wall."

"You can't see through the grime on the windows!"

"Relax, Clare. This isn't going to kill you."

"Probably not," she snapped. "I'll die of carbon monoxide poisoning first."

Sam laughed and reached for her. "You'd have to relax enough to breathe before the fumes could get you. Come on. My treat. What'll you have?"

Instead of backing away, Clare found herself leaning into the strength of Sam's body. He squeezed her shoulder and winked at her as he pulled her toward the small sliding glass window to place an order. When his hand slid lower to cup the curve of her waist, warning bells began to clang in Clare's head again. Almost nonchalantly, his fingers drifted beneath her jersey and rested against bare skin, his thumb casually rubbing tiny circles against her side.

The window slid open, and an orange-haired woman plopped a small green order pad on the counter. "Yeah?"

"I'll have the Super Split," Sam said. "With walnuts. And she'll have—"

"The . . . Raspberry Fudge Rhapsody," Clare said, and admitted to herself she had wanted one from the moment she read the neon starburst. She wet her lips in anticipation.

"You sure, honey? The Super Split's our Spring Fever Special this week," the woman explained tonelessly. "Buy one, get one free."

"Oh," murmured Clare. "In that case, give me one of those instead."

"No," Sam said immediately. The terse correction was a knee-jerk reaction, but all he could see in his mind was a picture of a quiet little orphan sitting in a restaurant, trying not to be a burden. *No, thank you. I don't want dessert. Really.* The tone of voice was the same one that he'd heard Clare use—so polite, so disappointed.

Sam shook his head at the woman and pulled his wallet out of his pocket. "Give the lady what she ordered."

When the window slid shut, Sam glared at Clare. "When you're with me, I expect you to order what *you* want, not what's easiest or cheapest."

Sam's tone brought Clare's chin up sharply. "Next time you're paying, I'll order one of everything. Excuse the hell out of me for being practical!"

"Practical? Hardly. I saw your face. I saw the conditioned response. I asked you once if you'd spent a lot of your life giving up things. You avoided the question. I'd bet my last dollar the answer was yes."

Heat rushed to her cheeks. To hide the flush, Clare glanced over her shoulder at an approaching couple. "You've been reading too damn many pop-psychology books."

Leaning over, Sam whispered, his breath fanning her cheek. "The only reading I've been doing is between the lines. And God help me, you fascinate me."

Startled by the husky promise in his voice, Clare drew in a sharp breath and swung her gaze to his. The uncertain yellow light cast shadows that darkened his eyes to black. When he didn't look away, her stomach gave the funny lurch it always gave when she found herself losing control. She wasn't having fun anymore. She didn't like the electrical charges that zipped along her nerves as he managed to hold her with nothing more than a look in his eyes.

She felt like an actress who'd been promised a wonderful part and then given a blank paper. She was supposed to be witty and charming and send him on his way with a pat on the head. Instead, she was tongue-tied and wanted to bury her fingers in his blond mane.

He wasn't supposed to make a troubled confession about finding her fascinating. But he had. The look in his eyes wasn't supposed to awaken the most unlikely places in her body. But it did. She wasn't supposed to want him to kiss her. But she wanted to, all right, and she was having trouble remembering why kissing Sam was a bad idea.

"You want napkins?" asked the woman as she slid two large containers of ice cream through the window.

"Please," Sam said, and finally turned away from

Clare. He grabbed their desserts and jerked his head toward the benches.

Relieved that the awkward moment had evaporated, Clare chose the concrete table farthest from the intersection and sat down. Sam slid in across from her and handed her the ice cream container, urging her to take it.

"I won't bite," he said. Then he added, "At least not until you're ready."

Audibly, Clare sucked in a breath, and then clamped her mouth shut.

Sam ferried a spoon of whipped cream, fudge, and strawberry to his mouth. "At least you have the good sense not to deny it anymore."

"Are you trying to make me uncomfortable?" Clare demanded. "Because you are. I'm as uncomfortable as hell. I don't know what's going on here. I don't have time for what's going on here. I don't even know where the assignment ends and you begin."

"Is that important?"

"Yes. No. I don't know."

With an effort, she dragged her gaze from his and concentrated on the sinfully rich raspberry sauce drizzled over hot fudge and French vanilla ice cream. Without hurrying, she let the spoon and its precious cargo glide into her mouth. She rolled the taste around on her tongue and closed her eyes before returning to the conversation. When she finished her first bite, she stared at him silently for a moment. Then she said, "You're not what I bargained for, Tucker."

"What? You think I phoned the Easter bunny and said, 'Hey, guy, please drop an impossible woman into my life. One who'll fit my body like I'd want a glove to fit! Give her a personality that says look but don't touch.

Oh, and by the way, make sure she's taking my class so I can worry about getting sued for sexual harassment.'" Sam glared at her and mined some more bananas from his container. "Bunnies cannot be trusted."

Stunned, Clare began to realize Sam's dilemma. He wanted to change her, and he wanted to jump her bones. Succeeding at one would probably cost him the other. His ethics were at war with his libido. The mighty Sam was human after all. Knowing that eased some of the anxiety in her gut.

Toying with her ice cream, Clare asked, "What are we going to do about this?"

Sam's ethics struggled with a healthy sex drive. Ethics won. "What do you want to do about this?"

"I don't know." Clare cocked her head and her brow as she slowly withdrew the pink plastic spoon from her mouth. "But I'm having fun again."

Sam almost choked when the spoon caught on her full lower lip, offering him a tantalizing sight of her tongue as it brushed against the cradle of the spoon. When Clare repeated the seductive performance with the next bite, Sam groaned and took his frustration out on his dish of ice cream.

She let him polish off several bites in silence. The final rays of daylight twisted through the sunset and accented the pale wheat and gold in his blond hair. The man was hold-your-breath gorgeous, and she knew that hair would feel like spun silk between her fingers. Before she did something foolish, she said, "Tell me about your class, Sam. Is that all you do, or do you have a real job too?"

"You don't consider the class a real job?"

"A six-week-long party is not a real job."

"Why do I get the feeling you disapprove of everything I do?"

"Of course I don't," Clare quipped with a grin. "You haven't told me everything you do yet."

Half finished with his banana split, Sam wiped his mouth and crumpled his napkin into a ball. "I'm a consultant."

"Don't tell me—let me guess. *The fun doctor.*"

Sam gave an exasperated sigh. "No, an export consultant for the Far East. Among other things, I help companies understand the nuances of Asian languages. Like communication in English, they can be filled with ambiguity."

"You?"

"Why is that so hard to believe?"

"I don't know." Clare shrugged and knitted her brows. "I guess I thought that dealing with Asian businessmen would require a . . . a more polished image."

Sam pretended to be offended. "And I'm not polished?"

"Maybe that's not the right word," Clare backpedaled and tried to put her impression of him into words. She couldn't see him in a power suit holding a Mont Blanc fountain pen. She couldn't see him with a day planner. All she could see was his killer smile and the mountain of chaos on his desk. "You're . . . well . . . rowdy."

Genuine amusement shook Sam as he realized that to Clare the word *rowdy* bordered on insult. "I guess I am—now anyway. Before you knew me, I was buttoned-down and bottled-up. Obsessed with my company and oblivious of life. Now I'm . . . rowdy."

"People don't change that much."

"You're right. People don't change. They rediscover parts of themselves they've lost."

"I don't need changing. I'm not lost," Clare said, knowing that his words were for her benefit.

"No, I think I've discovered you just in time." Sam's glance roved over her bare shoulder and back to her mouth.

Warmth spread through Clare's belly at the thought of Sam discovering anything about her. She imagined his strong hands and fingers as he explored her body. *Sam.* When had he become Sam and not Tucker? Her libido supplied the answer—*the moment you started thinking about his hands.* When a man puts his hands on a woman's body, it's time to drop the last name.

"Gosh, look at the time," Clare said suddenly, ignoring his comment and the meaningful look he tossed in her direction. She slipped the errant edge of her jersey back over her shoulder. "You promised you'd have me home early."

"So I did," agreed Sam, and checked his watch. "But it's still early. Mickey's little hand is only halfway between the seven and the eight."

"That's late." Clare's comment brooked no argument. She scraped the sides of her ice cream container and popped the last bite in her mouth. "Ellie's coming. I have to clean house. Besides, it's getting dark."

"It was dark fifteen minutes ago," Sam corrected her helpfully.

"Look, Sam, are you going to take me home or not?"

"Sure. Unless you want to lick your bowl before we leave?"

Horrified, Clare realized she had eaten the raspberry

chocolate concoction much the same way a starving man might have eaten fresh-baked bread. Defensively, Clare said, "It was good."

"Uh-huh," he agreed. "See what you've been missing?"

"I haven't been missing ice cream."

"Then why didn't you argue about where to go? Haven't you got a favorite spot?" When Clare didn't answer, he prodded, "Can you even name an establishment that sells ice cream?"

"The grocery store," Clare snapped.

"Right." Sam nodded his head sadly.

Clare tossed her trash into the double-sized bin and pressed her lips together. Cheerful men annoyed her. Especially when they were right. She didn't go out for ice cream, but that was beside the point. "Stop analyzing me, Sam. Or is that the one thing you haven't been able to change about yourself?"

"That and an attraction to impossible women."

"Take me home, Sam."

"Yes, ma'am."

He walked her to the car, held her door open, all the while brushing his hand against her back, her shoulder, and elbow as he helped her in. Finally, Clare said, "I can manage!"

"Yes, ma'am." Sam walked around, got in the car, and started the engine without saying anything else. After Sam pulled the car into the street, he asked, "Who's Ellie? Three seconds after you mention her name, you start cleaning house again. Is she coming to see you or eat off your floor?"

"She's my cousin—" Clare paused and told the truth.

"And I haven't the faintest idea why she's coming. I haven't seen her in five years."

Clare's flat tone was a not-so-subtle warning to drop the discussion about Ellie. Taking the hint, he steered the conversation to safer topics. Not that it mattered now. The damage was done. She'd overreacted, and he'd filed Ellie away for future consideration. As usual, her cousin was gone but not forgotten.

When the Volvo slowed to a stop in her parking lot, Clare jumped out, murmured her thanks, and slammed the door. She was halfway up the walk and congratulating herself for having survived the evening with only minor dents in her social armor, when she heard the telltale clunk of his door opening.

"A southern gentleman always sees a lady to the door."

"Of course," Clare said, rolling her eyes in disgust before she continued toward her condo. "I should have known."

"Known what?" The humor in his voice was barely disguised.

"That you wouldn't rest until I promised to show up for class tomorrow."

Sam stopped suddenly, but not just because they'd reached her door. He began to wonder how much of the evening was an act for his benefit and how much was the real Clare. "Were you planning on ditching?"

Clare retrieved her keys from her purse and opened the door just wide enough to toss her purse inside. "The thought had crossed my mind. I thought you might cut me some slack since I've been such a good sport about tonight."

"If I give you any more rope," Sam said pleasantly,

even though his eyes flashed dangerously, "you'll probably hang us both."

"Dammit, Sam. You don't understand. Right now is
not a good time for me. The budget's overdue. I've got a
new computer system to deal with, and—"

"Ellie's coming," he finished for her. "I don't care if
the President is coming for breakfast. You will be at class
tomorrow, or you can explain why to Dave. Not that it
will help, considering his frame of mind, but you can give
it a shot."

"Fine." Clare jerked the keys out of the lock. "I'll be
there. Satisfied?"

"No," Sam answered softly, checking his anger. "I
want *you* to show up tomorrow. Not the dog-and-pony
show you trot out to fool the general public. I want
something real."

Before she could slip away from him, Sam reached
out to hook a finger in the neckline of her jersey, pulling
her toward him. Objectively, Sam knew he was using his
anger as an excuse to justify what he'd wanted to do since
the first time he'd seen Clare McGuire. But that didn't
make a difference. He intended to kiss Clare. He needed
to—had to. And he knew that kissing her would compli-
cate his life. That didn't make a difference either.

Part of Clare wanted Sam to hurry up and get it over
with, and the other part of her savored the anticipation,
the illusion that time had stopped and reality had narrowed to the feel of his hands on her bare skin as he drew
her into the warmth of his body.

When Sam had settled her against his chest, he let go
of her jersey and brushed the skin below her neck with
the backs of his fingers. For a moment he toyed with the

hollow at the base of her throat, his attention absorbed by the creamy softness his thumb discovered. Then he burrowed his fingers in her hair, cradling her head. Finally, he tilted her face to suit himself and kissed her.

FOUR

Clare had been kissed before, but never like this. Never with such complete possession. Sam didn't kiss. He branded. His tongue traced the curve of her lips and urged her mouth open. Anticipation surged through her as his tongue delved into her mouth, finding and coaxing a response from its mate. Each swirl of his tongue spun sensation through her belly, and her nipples tightened when his hand slipped under her jersey to explore her back and press her closer.

A strangled, panicked sound escaped her throat, and she pulled her mouth from his. Closing her eyes, she tried to unjumble her emotions, to regain control, but Sam fed hungrily on her bottom lip, pulling it gently between his teeth, teasing and bathing it with his tongue. Her own body encouraged him by leaning into his hardness and molding to his desire. His cologne was utterly masculine and assaulted her senses, reminding her of winter fires and brandy. Finally, Clare gave in to the sensation building inside her, and opened her mouth to Sam's insistence, inviting the heat of his kiss.

When Clare surrendered, Sam let his mouth seal hers in earnest, plunging his tongue into the velvet welcome. This was the Clare he wanted—open and giving. He would never forget his first taste of her, all chocolate and raspberry. When he lifted his head, he gently held her back. He wanted to see desire in her eyes. He wanted to see a part of Clare that was only for him. Slowly, her lids lifted and her hands crept up on the front of his shirt. Confusion and passion stared at him from eyes that were midnight blue in the darkness. God, she was beautiful. He wondered if she even knew that. He decided her lips were more enticing swollen from his kisses than they had been before.

His voice was rusty when he spoke. "You have two choices, Clare. You can stand here in the open doorway all night, in which case the cat gets out." He paused to feather her short, thick hair with his fingers. "Or you can invite me in."

Still sorting through the sensual overload caused by his kiss, Clare shook her head to clear the gossamer cobwebs woven around her logic and murmured, "Slick doesn't . . . get out. He hates the outdoors."

Chuckling, Sam propelled her backward. "Right now, I do too. Invite me inside."

"No!" Clare's head suddenly cleared. Cobwebs disappeared. No matter how *interesting* Tucker's kisses were, he wasn't coming in. That would be disastrous in more ways than one. Letting him inside her house was one step closer to letting him in her life. And that she refused to do. Six weeks, she reminded herself. Six weeks of Tuesday nights and Saturday mornings was all she was willing to give Tucker. It was all she had to give a man like Tucker. A man who had everything didn't need "poor Clare."

And she didn't need his casual touch and clever smile. She didn't need the warmth of his embrace. She needed to hold on to the one constant fact in her life—if she didn't let people get close, she wouldn't hurt so bad when they walked away. She pressed one hand against his chest and pushed. "Thank you for a lovely evening. Good night."

Even as she spoke, Clare stepped back and shut the door. Sam didn't need a mirror to tell him the expression on his face was complete and total shock. He cocked a hip and crossed his arms over his chest. "This is a helluva good-bye!" he complained to the closed door. "Here's your hat. What's your hurry?"

Silence greeted his sarcasm.

"Tomorrow, McGuire," he reminded her, and started toward his car. Absently, he rubbed his bottom lip with his thumb. *If Slick didn't get out, then why the contortionist act earlier?*

"No, Dave."

"Yes, Clare."

"Why?" It was more of a plea than a question.

"Because we need him. I've never exported auto parts to the East! I don't talk the lingo or understand the protocol in a deal like this. Hell, knowing me, I'd probably insult an Asian businessman just by pointing to a chair and saying 'Take a load off!' "

"You're not that bad."

"I know car parts. I'm not subtle, and I never will be. But I'm not stupid. That's why I hired Sam. He knows how to do business outside the southern good ol' boy network. Half the time, *yes* is *no* in the Far East. This is our chance to hit it big. Think about it for a minute. Take your time." Dave gave her his smug I'm-the-boss-and-we-both-know-I'm-right smile. "I'll wait right here in your office while you think."

Clare kept her head from exploding by grabbing her skull and pushing as hard as she could. If only the same technique would keep her life from disintegrating as well. Work got farther behind every day because Dave insisted she leave at five o'clock sharp. Ellie had yet to finalize her plans beyond a nebulous "soon." The new computer system had a glitch. A one-hundred-thousand-dollar custom-designed glitch and a programmer who didn't exactly inspire confidence with his assessment of the situation, which was, "No problem—I think."

And now . . . *now* Dave had succeeded in making her life impossible by jumping into bed with Japanese auto manufacturers and inviting Tucker to the pajama party. She didn't know if her peace of mind could take any more of Sam Tucker. He haunted her, hounded her, taunted her, excited her. Pick a verb and he did it to her. For two weeks she'd suffered through classes and assignments with Tucker, facing the fire she saw in his eyes and trying to ignore the fire that flared inside her.

Even now she panicked when she thought of the kiss. Losing herself in Tucker's arms had scared the hell out of her. Rightly so. She'd never lost that edge before, never lost sight of where she ended and the other person began. She didn't want excitement. She wanted dependable. She wanted safe.

Look, Tucker, the kiss was nice—

When she'd said that the next morning, Tucker's eyebrows went skyward. Then he laughed a deep rumble of a laugh that made her stomach flip-flop. "Nice?" he questioned, one eyebrow still in orbit. And then he called her McGuire again. Just as he had the night before. "McGuire, I don't know your frame of reference on the subject, but you can trust me on this one. That was one helluva kiss."

Tucker, you don't understand. This isn't what I want. I don't have time for this. For you.

For an instant, his eyes had dulled as if he were remembering something painful. Then he produced a throwaway smile and agreed to forget the kiss had ever happened.

At least she thought he had. Now, instead of straightforward lust, an undercurrent of tension rippled in the air at unexpected moments. No denying they struck a spark off each other. More than that. Tucker struck a nerve. She fought him every step of the way on every assignment, but he always managed to find out more about her than she was willing to tell.

Learning to relax was making her a nervous wreck. She couldn't keep her guard up constantly, and when her defenses slipped, Tucker stepped in. While they were together, Clare usually forgot that he was systematically turning her neat, organized routine upside down.

Their opinions didn't always agree, and there was something seductive about sparring. Because they weren't really arguing about the world. They were arguing about the primitive push-pull that drew men and women together. Beneath everything there was the hunger in his eyes, the hunger in her soul. She'd forgotten about that—the hunger, the tiny space inside her that wanted to be a part of somebody else's heart. And she'd forgotten how addictive fun could be.

Dragging herself back to the problem at hand, Clare let go of her head when she was certain it wasn't going to shatter. She looked at Dave and tried to compromise. "Give Stuart the project. He and Sam are fly-by-the-seat-of-their-pants guys."

Dave flung his hands in the air and snorted. "Right. Like I'm going to let a sales manager put together numbers for the bid. You and I both know that Stuart can't figure cost to save his soul, and he'll promise the moon to close the sale! You're the only one I trust to put this deal together. A deal we can live with, make a profit on, and actually have a shot at producing on schedule."

Sensing an opportunity, Clare decided it was time to make Dave swallow some of the platitudes he'd been handing out so readily the last few weeks. "I'm just one person, Dave. I can't do it all. Not with my schedule."

His eyes narrowed suspiciously. "What are you driving at?"

"I'm not driving at anything. I'm flat telling you. My dance card's full."

"Then sit out a few dances!" Dave roared.

"Fine by me," Clare roared right back, suddenly angry. "But I'm dancing to your tune! What do you suggest I do? Drop Tucker's class? Forget about the computer and go back to stone tablets and chisels? Ignore the fact that purchasing exceeds their budget on a regular basis? Tell the bank I don't have time to discuss our new credit line? Or maybe I should tell the cousin I haven't seen in five years that now is not a good time for a visit. Maybe she could reschedule for next year!"

Dave couldn't have looked more stunned if she'd

taken a two-by-four and whacked him square in the face. When he finally spoke, he said, "Touché! I guess I had that coming."

Wisely, Clare said nothing. She hadn't meant to shout, but she wasn't sorry. Dave didn't hold grudges, and this wasn't the first shouting match he'd been known to have. With any luck, it wouldn't be the last. Belatedly Clare realized that two weeks before, she wouldn't have dreamed of shouting at Dave. Decorum had been her motto for so long, she'd forgotten her mother called her Quick because she'd had a short fuse as a young child and had been quick to anger. Maybe Sam was right. People didn't change. They just rediscovered parts of themselves.

A half grunt, half sigh escaped Dave as he dropped into a chair. A companionable silence settled around them. "I guess I'm as much to blame as you for your workaholic tendencies."

Clare grinned. "Let's just say you nurture them."

"I need you on this project."

"I know. But that means you can't boot me out the door at five, and I'm going to have to skip Mr. Tucker's Saturdays." Clare waited for him to absorb what she'd said. Then she dropped the other shoe. "Tomorrow's Saturday."

He didn't look happy, but when he heaved himself out of the chair, Dave said, "I'll talk to him. Maybe you can try the class again on the next go-round."

"Mmmm," Clare murmured noncommittally.

As Dave left her office, her intercom buzzed.

Clare ignored the intercom and shouted through the open door, "What is it, Joshua?"

"While you were yell—I mean talking to Dave, a lady

called." His voice got louder as he walked toward her door. Leaning in, he pushed his glasses up and said, "She hung up before I could get her name. Sounded all out of breath and wouldn't leave a number. Said to tell you she was rushing to catch a plane and she'd see you tomorrow."

"She said *what*?" Terror flooded every crevice of Clare's awareness.

Patiently, Joshua repeated his message and added, "Delta Airlines. Seven forty-five. She said not to be late. She hates waiting."

"Go away!" Clare yelled at the insistent knock on the door and simultaneously grabbed a stack of newspapers, cringing at the two-week-old date. When the knock repeated, she stopped cleaning long enough to wrench open the door. "I'm not buying cookies, magazines or—Tucker!"

"Bad time?" Sam asked. The question didn't need an answer. She looked like hell, didn't have shoes on, and had a dust rag over one shoulder, but he thought she was sexy. Of course, given the state of his suppressed libido, Clare could have been wearing an army tent and a paper bag over her head and he'd have still thought she was sexy. The past two weeks had been fun, but two weeks of looking and not touching had taken their toll. Sam jammed his hands in his back pockets to control the urge to reach out for her. His senses remembered all too well how soft and pliant she was in his arms.

Clare sputtered and clutched the newspapers to her chest. "I can't be in the class anymore. Didn't Dave call you?"

"Yes."

"Then why are you here?"

"Do I have to have a reason? Can't a friend want to see another friend? You told me I couldn't kiss you, but you didn't say I couldn't be your friend."

Warily, Clare studied Sam. He was wearing those disreputable cut-up jeans and a disarming expression. Trouble, she decided, and knew she had to end the conversation before Sam got her all tangled up in knots. She didn't like the funny way he emphasized the word *friend*. This was how it always started. An innocent question from Sam, and then like a bolt from the blue he zapped her and had her admitting to everything but Jimmy Hoffa's disappearance. She wasn't going to get pulled in this time.

"No, you do not have to have a reason to see me." Clare shifted the bundle in her arms. "But according to Ann Landers, if you don't call first, I don't have to let you in. Here." She thrust the newspapers into his hands. "At least make yourself useful. Toss these in the Dumpster on your way to the Volvo."

She started to shut the door, but Sam wedged his white leather Reebok between the door and the jamb. Sighing, she said, "Sam, I don't have time tonight."

His deep brown eyes mocked her. "You say that entirely too often, you know. You should break the habit. Or at least come up with a better excuse. And don't tell me the one about having to clean house because Ellie's coming."

Clare made a strangled sound. "Ellie *is* coming. To-morrow. Now, could you get your foot out of my door?"

"Not until you tell me why you're so twisted about

Ellie's visit? How long could it take to fluff a few pillows?"

Gritting her teeth, Clare let the door swing wide. The only way to get rid of him was to let him glimpse the magnitude of her problem. Admitting defeat graciously was not her strong suit, but she stepped aside and waved him in with a short, jerky motion. "Fluffing pillows is the least of my worries. It's the rest of the place that has me concerned."

Vaguely thankful that he couldn't see the kitchen or the downstairs bathroom from his vantage point, Clare tried to look at the scene objectively, laying bets with herself as to what would draw his attention first. The decor was early garage sale. Her laundry spanned the long hallway in piles haphazardly sorted by color. Counted cross-stitch paraphernalia from an unfinished project littered the coffee table, as did a collection of soft drink cans and plastic microwave dinner plates. *Maybe she could say she was recycling?*

In a whimsical mood she'd written her name in the dust on the top of the television. A string of red lights in the shape of chili peppers still hung cheerfully around the outline of her hallway. She'd forgotten to take them down after Christmas. All of these things stood out amid the general clutter, but the one overwhelming embarrassment was the black lace bra Slick alternately attacked and dragged around the room. Clare narrowed her eyes and plotted cat revenge.

"Cute cat," Sam said, and enjoyed the show. Elation shot through him. He felt like an amateur slob in the presence of a master. Raising his head heavenward, Sam murmured gratefully, "Yes, Virginia, there is a Santa Claus." Then more loudly and with enjoyment in every word, he said, "Clare McGuire, you hypocrite. You're not as perfect as you pretend. You're a first class slob."

"It's *my* house. I like it this way," she said stiffly. She did. When she moved away from her aunt and uncle, she decided she'd have a home, not a house filled with "things." A living, breathing home that swallowed her with welcome when she walked in the door. A home that didn't judge her by how neatly she kept the medicine cabinet. A home that said "I belong to you."

Clare held open the door. "Now, if you're through laughing at my expense, could you take the papers to the Dumpster and leave me alone. I've got work to do."

Together they said, "Ellie's coming."

A muscle twitched at the corner of Clare's mouth. The grin on Sam's face broadened as he looked pointedly around. "Get some plastic explosives and save yourself some time."

Clare refused to laugh or even admit that Sam had lightened her mood. She ignored the connection her mind made between seeing Sam and feeling happy. "Thanks for the household hint, Tucker, but I don't think it will come to that. If you really want to help me, say good night."

Clearing a space on the coffee table, Sam dumped the papers. "I really want to help. What can I do first?"

"I've already told you. Take those papers to the Dumpster!" she said in exasperation.

"I'm not stupid, Clare. Once you get me out the door, you won't let me back in. Stop being so stubborn." He looked around again, but without any disapproval in his expression. "You need all the help you can get. What time is Ellie coming?"

Clare slammed the door and leaned against it. Sam had a way of slicing right to the problem. "Tomorrow."

"When tomorrow?"

"Seven forty-five."

"In the morning?" Sam asked as he gingerly lifted the top of a cardboard pizza box.

"I don't know. Joshua didn't find out," Clare snapped, suddenly cross. Pushing away from the door, she scooped up the pizza box with enough force to smack the lid shut. Clare deposited the box in a large, dark-green plastic lawn bag beside the overstuffed armchair.

"That's not true," she corrected him. "It wasn't Joshua's fault. Ellie didn't bother to tell him. I called the airline and there's a flight arriving at seven thirty-five A.M. and one arriving at seven-fifty P.M. But nothing at seven forty-five!" She gave the box a good shove to flatten the other trash, and under her breath she added, "Ellie never remembers details. She never had to."

"Hey," Sam called softly, and swung her around to face him. This time he was sure he heard resentment in her voice, and he wasn't going to let her go until he had some answers to the questions that had begun to nag his subconscious. "What did Ellie do to you that ties you up in knots?"

"Specifically or generally?" Clare quipped, and looked away, wishing she'd guarded her words. Letting Sam inside had been a mistake. As soon as he'd touched her, she knew he wouldn't settle for flip retorts or clever evasions. Lifting her gaze to his, she waited.

Sam concentrated on banishing every trace of desire in his touch. He intended the gentle rubbing of his thumbs on the round curve of her shoulder to be comforting, relaxing, but his fingertips had ideas of their own. Now is not the time, he told himself firmly. Her blue eyes were troubled. Whatever caused the tension between the cousins, Clare obviously felt guilty about it. When the muscles beneath his fingers began to relax, he asked, "Do you like Ellie?"

"Wrong question," Clare answered, and pulled away from him. "Everybody likes her. She's one in a million. A golden girl with a silver spoon. She's Ellie Jordan."

The name stirred a flash of awareness in Sam's brain, and then the full impact of the name settled into his consciousness. The words *swimsuit issue* and Ellie Jordan were synonymous. "You're kidding."

"Would I kid about a woman who's graced more magazine covers than British royalty? And, yes, I know we don't look anything alike."

Slick yowled at Sam's feet and demanded attention. Sam hunkered down and rubbed the cat behind the ears. "Is that why you're mad at her?"

Startled by his question, Clare stopped in the middle of gathering up soda cans from the table. She took a long time to answer the question. Thoughtfully, she let the cans slide from her hands into the garbage bag. "I'm not mad at her."

Her conscience pinched her, and Clare added, "At least, not because she's a model."

Loud purring reached a crescendo and then diminished, only to begin again. Sam angled his head to study Clare. From the floor he got an interesting view of the legs that had fascinated him from the first night he met her. Black stretch pants flowed over every muscle, every soft curve, and molded to her in a way that made Sam ache. He compared her to his recollection of Ellie Jordan and decided he liked short, vulnerable brunettes more than he liked leggy blondes in skimpy spandex swimsuits.

Her pants didn't reach her ankles, and Sam found the bared skin as alarmingly provocative as the knowledge that her lingerie tastes included black lace. Clearing his throat, he stood back up and solemnly handed Clare the bra he'd retrieved from Slick's neck. "Why are you mad at Ellie?"

Clare snatched the bra from his fingers, heat flaming her cheeks. "Because she was always first."

Surprised, Sam said, "First? Like the first to have a boyfriend? The first to graduate? The first to make a million dollars?"

"The first one my uncle hugged when he came home." Clare lifted her chin, and her eyes glittered. "Are you happy now? I've admitted it. I'm jealous of something that isn't even Ellie's fault."

Sam made no comment as he reached out and tucked her short hair behind her ears. Every fiber in his body was screaming for him to pull her into his arms, but his mind knew better. Clare would only interpret that as pity. She wasn't the kind of woman who wanted pity. She didn't let go of her secrets easily. Her admission was probably only the tip of the iceberg.

Realizing she still held the black lace bra, Clare rolled her eyes and shook her head. "Sam, I really don't have time for you to play Sigmund Freud right now. I've got a lot to do and very little time to do it."

"Then you should be thanking me for offering to help."

"God, give me strength," Clare whispered, and gave Sam what she hoped was an evil look. "You probably don't have the faintest idea what to do. How to clean. You're a man. You grew up with a mother and a butler."

"And you are a reverse chauvinist." Sam picked up a crumpled ball of paper from the coffee table. Expertly, he flipped it behind his back and into the garbage bag.

Throwing up her hands, Clare said, "What the hell. You clean the downstairs, and I'll take the upstairs. The kitchen, a half-bath, and dining room are down that hallway. Cleaning supplies are in the kitchen, and the vacuum is in the laundry alcove across from the kitchen. Got it?" When Sam nodded, she added, "Whoever gets through first starts on the patio."

Sam held out his hand. "May the best man win."

"This isn't a contest." Clare frowned and realized that Sam was back to touching her at every opportunity. "Are you sure?"

"Go upstairs and don't come down until you're through," Sam answered. When she finally left, he turned his attention to the living room. Throw pillows crowded the couch and spilled into the floor. After he rearranged the cushions, Sam tried tossing the small, colorful pillows onto the sofa. Instead of falling in artistic disarray, the pillows sagged and drooped pitifully in piles of mush.

Sam chewed on his lip. He'd never seen pillows more in need of fluffing than these. Purposefully, he gathered them all up and shoved them into the dryer. For a moment his hand hovered indecisively over the timer as he wondered how long pillows took to fluff. Shrugging, he turned the dial to ninety minutes.

By the time he "uncluttered" the living room, dusted the dining room, put a load of towels in the washer, and vacuumed, Sam decided that William and Rebecca probably deserved raises. An hour later Sam gave the freshly mopped and waxed kitchen floor a nod of approval. His part of the house was definitely beginning to shape up.

The dryer hummed faintly behind him, and he remembered the pillows. Whistling, he reached for the dryer door and pulled it open. Every self-satisfied thought in his head evaporated as an explosion of white and gray feathers erupted from the dryer and shot into the kitchen. His mouth dropped open, and he was too horrified to do more than curse as the dryer tumbled around again and dispensed more feathers. Belatedly, he thought of slamming the dryer door and then cursed again as the whoosh of air sent feathers swirling into the living room and pushed them farther into the kitchen.

"Sonofa—" Sam began, and stopped. *This is a nightmare.* He watched feathers commit suicide by drifting toward his waxed kitchen floor, peppering his nice, shiny surface, and sticking to the wet wax.

"I'm a dead man," Sam whispered as he imagined what Clare's response would be. He shut his eyes briefly, but when he opened them again, feathers still swirled in the air. Sam hung his head as the air conditioner decided to kick in and sent cool air roaring out of the vents. The downstairs looked like someone had picked it up and shaken it like a snow globe. *How many feathers could six pillows hold, for God's sake?*

Desperately, he began chasing the feathers that floated toward the stairway at the back of the hall. His hands resembled goldfish gulping at food. While he snatched feathers from the air, he made up and discarded excuses for the mess. Expertly, he plucked a large speckled feather from the air and deposited it in his pocket for safekeeping.

He'd almost convinced himself that Clare would see the humor in the situation, when he heard her footsteps on the stairs. Swearing, he stepped into the stairwell and smiled what he hoped was an innocent smile. "What did you say?"

Clare stopped. "I didn't say anything."

"Oh! Thought you did. Well, now that I'm here, don't bother to come down. I'll get what you need. What do you need?"

"A glass of water," Clare said, and drew her brows together. Unease blossomed in her stomach as she watched a feather rock back and forth in the air and finally settle on Sam's shoulder.

FIVE

Suddenly the faint smell of burning feathers slipped up the stairwell. Clare's knees buckled, and she sat down heavily on the steps, afraid to go any farther. For the last hour she'd begun to believe that Ellie's visit might be all right. That she could just confess to "fudging a bit" when she'd described her new place. But her first whiff of scorched feathers had cruelly snatched that dream away. This was all her fault for lying in the first place. For trying to pretend that she wasn't poor Clare anymore.

"Oh, my God. What have you done, Tucker?"

Sam looked behind him and then apologetically back at her. He held one hand out as though to stop her. "Nothing that William can't fix."

His words sent her heart plummeting toward her toes and galvanized her into action. With every step, the smell of singed feathers became stronger. By the time she reached Sam, she wanted to wring his neck.

Wisely, Sam stepped out of her way. Sam thought he was watching a slow motion movie as Clare pulled the dryer open, dispensing more feathers as she retrieved an empty pillow cover. Sam expected anger or tears, but when she finally turned around, her face was devoid of expression.

"Ellie's coming tomorrow," Clare said matter-of-factly.

Feeling like a heel, Sam tried to reassure not only Clare but himself as well. "I'll call William. We'll fix this." Guilt flooded Sam as he tried to gather her in his arms. "Promise."

"Promise!" Clare thumped his chest with enough force to send him back a pace. "Do you know how long I'll be finding feathers?"

Sam slipped his hand into his pocket, guiltily fingering the feathers he'd stuffed inside. "I tried to help."

"Next time don't help," Clare said as she walked into the kitchen. She needed aspirin. Several aspirin. "Oh, my God."

"I waxed the floor," Sam said even though the scene in the kitchen was fairly self-explanatory. "I may have used a little too much wax."

Gingerly, Clare retraced her steps, grimacing as her bare feet touched the surface of sticky wax and smooth feathers. Once again in the hallway, Clare spared a glare for Sam and then inspected the bottom of her feet. Speckled feathers clung to her feet. Hundreds were still firmly attached to the kitchen floor. *God, what a mess.*

"Let's think this through logically," Sam began, but Clare interrupted.

"What is it with men and logic? Logic isn't going to help." Clare pushed away from the door frame and walked into the living room. "Unless logic can magically turn this condominium into a house with a big yard. Unless logic can miraculously replace my antique quilted pillows. Unless logic can erase the Roseanne decorating style."

Confused, Sam followed her and asked, "What's wrong with Roseanne?"

Clare slumped into the armchair. "Nothing. Not a thing. Except I told Ellie and her parents that I did my new placc in antiques."

Sam looked around and raised an eyebrow. "You lied."

Frowning, Clare said defensively, "Not exactly. I *was* going to furnish the place with antiques, but the pillows were as far as I got. It didn't make much sense to waste money on antiques until I needed new furniture."

Slick yowled in agitation as Sam woke him and shoved him off the sofa. The cat's protest stopped abruptly as his nose twitched, and he froze with his limbs in stalking position. The cat began to rumble a sound so deep and quiet, Sam wasn't sure it was a sound at all. Sam leaned back into the sofa as the cat began to adjust his crouch position, reminding him of a race car inching up to the starting line.

"Is this normal behavior for him?" Sam asked in amusement.

Clare shot him a withering look as Slick attacked a bit of gossamer floating by. "What'd you expect? His house is full of feathers." Clare reached down to pick Slick up, but he bound away. "He's going to keep Ellie up nights growling and stalking and pouncing. Ellie hates cats."

"Is that why you got one?"

The question slid into her belly and twisted as painfully as any knife would have. *Was that why she got a cat?* Because Ellie had never liked cats? Unconsciously, she pulled her feet up onto the easy chair and wrapped her arms around her knees. Sam continually held up a mirror to her soul, and sometimes she didn't like her reflection.

Finally, she looked at Sam and hated that she cared what he thought of her. But she did. Her awareness of him hummed beneath the surface of every gesture and every question. This is what she always knew would happen if she let someone get too close. She wouldn't be able to keep her secrets anymore.

What would Sam think of her when he found out that the last thing she said to her parents was "I hope you go away and never come back!" The memory taunted her, and the familiar fingers of guilt closed coldly around her heart. Adult rationalization reminded her that a seven-year-old, upset about being left with a baby-sitter, wasn't to blame for the auto accident.

She steeled herself for Sam's disapproval and said, "I bought Slick because I wanted company. And because I knew a cat would drive Ellie crazy if she ever visited."

Instead of censure, Sam laughed aloud and gave her a thumbs-up. "Excellent."

Startled, Clare unwrapped her arms and crossed her legs yoga-style so she could lean forward. "Didn't you hear me? I just said that I'm a petty person. I chose a cat for a pet simply because I knew it would annoy Ellie."

Sam's grin was almost infectious. "So? I once bought a snake because I knew it would drive my sister wild."

Nonplussed, Clare stared at him for a moment. She didn't know what his game was, but she wasn't about to be talked out of her guilt by a few smooth words. "Child-hood pranks don't count."

"I bought the snake last year for my nephew's birth-day." Sam stretched his legs out, obviously pleased with himself. "I thought Pamela was being a little ridiculous about the kids getting a pet that constantly shed hair all over her house, so I got the snake."

"That's rotten!"

"Hey, she's the one who wanted a low-maintenance pet. Snakes shed their skin all at once." Sam spread his hands in a what-more-could-you-ask-for gesture. "Easy cleanup."

Torn between laughter and outrage, Clare's mood suddenly lightened, and she grinned. Sam's warm brown eyes bathed her with approval, and his approval warmed her from the inside out. If Sam could saddle his sister with a snake, then buying a cat because Ellie didn't like them wasn't such a horribly mean-spirited action. It wasn't as if Ellie were allergic. Besides, Ellie's European travel schedule had made the likelihood of a visit remote. Until now.

Unable to resist, Clare asked, "Does your nephew still have the snake?"

"No. Pamela promptly revised her position on furry pets when she found out the snake had to be fed two live mice each week."

"And any good mother knows, you can't just take away a boy's pet. It's un-American," Clare said as comprehension dawned.

"Unless you make a trade," Sam suggested smugly. "A golden retriever named Monster is now king of the castle."

"I've always suspected you were the sneaky sort."

Sam stood up and managed an affronted expression. "I prefer to think of myself as the subtle sort." He ignored her attempt to contradict him. "It's time to call William for help."

"William," Clare echoed, and looked apprehensively

around. As always, Sam had managed to make her forget her problems. Cleaning the house was only a Band-Aid cure for the mess she was in. Over the years she'd made enough misleading statements about her lifestyle to create an inescapable trap for herself. The time had come to pay the piper. This was her responsibility, not Sam's. Or William's. She'd figure a way out of this mess.

"Thanks, but no thanks," Clare said, reaching for the Yellow Pages in the magazine rack by her chair. "I'll call in the real cleaning professionals."

"Face it, Clare. You're not going to get anyone to come out on a Friday ni—"

The rest of Sam's words were drowned out as catastrophe struck again. The sounds of a feline World War III assailed their ears. Slick bawled out a horrid exorcist sound that finished with a caterwaul punctuated by china crashing to the floor. Sam and Clare stared at each other with widened eyes and then bolted for the kitchen, jamming the doorway. They arrived in time to see Slick clinging desperately to the window curtains. He began to slip, his claws leaving a trail in the sheer fabric.

Risking a sideways look at Clare, Sam saw the blood drain from her face as the curtain rod bowed and finally came off the wall from the strain. A small chunk of plasterboard came off with the rod, leaving an ugly black hole. Slick squalled as he hit the sticky floor, jumping up, turning flips, and running sideways, trying to shake the feathers off his paws.

An instinctive reluctance to enter the melee held them both rooted in place. Finally Sam stepped into the kitchen and bent to scoop up Slick. "Hold on, partner. I'll get you."

Slick hissed and whipped his tail, but he allowed Sam

to pick him up after one reproachful meow at Clare, who turned and headed for the bathroom. Sam wasn't sure whether she was going to be ill or if she was getting a warm washcloth for Slick's feet. Gingerly picking his way, he left the kitchen and stood uncomfortably in the hallway. He held Slick slightly away from his body and said, "Thanks a lot, pal. I may have turned on the heat, but you've managed to finish cooking my goose."

When Clare emerged from the bathroom, her mouth was set in a grim line, and she carried a teal-colored washcloth. Immediately, Sam shifted the cat and presented his paws to Clare, who bent her head and gently began to clean. For some reason, the top of her head made Sam feel guilty. "This isn't as bad as it looks. We can fix the wall."

Looking up at him without raising her head, Clare gave him some valuable advice. "Quit while you're behind, Tucker."

"The name's Sam, and you've got to loosen up, Clare. This is one of those slices of life that creates an unforgettable memory. There are public speakers all across the country who would kill for an anecdote like this."

"Would they kill you specifically?" asked Clare sweetly.

"Why does your house have to be perfect, Clare? Why do *you* have to be perfect, for that matter? Are you ashamed of how you live?"

Clare finished Slick's paws and rubbed his pelt down with the cloth. "I'm not ashamed. I don't want more for me," she said quietly, and took the cat from him. "They—my aunt and uncle and Ellie—want more for me. They don't understand how anyone could be happy without a country estate and gobs of servants."

Instinctively, Sam knew Clare was about to give him the piece of the puzzle he'd been trying to find for weeks. She hugged the cat and was silent for a moment before continuing.

"You never had to be grateful for anything. At least not for the roof over your head, the clothes you wore, even the food you ate." Clare set Slick down and watched him race upstairs. "You never had to be *poor Clare.* Well, I did. And I hated it. I never meant to lie to my aunt and uncle. I said one thing, and they assumed another."

Clare took aim and sent the washcloth arrowing toward the kitchen sink before continuing. "What they assumed made them happy. They didn't have to be responsible for poor Clare anymore. She was doing fine, wonderful in fact. I can just hear what they say when their friends ask about me: "Why, she'd bought the kind of house one furnishes in antiques! Little Clare is a hotshot with some big automotive company." I didn't correct them because it felt so *good* not to be poor Clare anymore. I didn't see the need to tell them when the automotive company was barely turning a profit."

Once again Sam was forced to put his hands in his pockets for fear that he'd grab her to kiss the hurt away. "Surely you didn't think you could keep up the charade?"

Clare laughed hollowly and looked up at him. "Why not? My aunt's health keeps her from traveling. My uncle won't leave her, and Ellie's always busy in Europe with the jet-setting."

"Not anymore," Sam noted gently.

"Not anymore," Clare echoed, and dragged a hand through her hair. "And unless I can convince Ellie I'm doing great, my uncle will start trying to send money again. Do you have any idea what it feels like to take their money? They don't love me; they throw money just to ease the guilt. They don't understand that I like living here."

"And you thought cleaning up the place would fool your cousin? Darlin', to convince Ellie, you need a real house, or you'll go back to being poor Clare." Abruptly, Clare fixed him with an intent gaze. Sam could actually see the lightbulb switch on over her head, and he took a step away. "Wait a minute—"

"No, don't you see!" Clare advanced on him, suddenly a woman with a purpose. "That's the answer—all I need is a house like yours. *Exactly* like yours. It'll be for only a few days. A week at the most. I'll pay you."

As soon as Sam heard the proposition, his libido was screaming, *Yes! Just where I want her! In my house!* The newly acquired sparkle in her eyes was enticing, but he knew better than to give in to his lust. Sharing a house with Clare would be a disaster. He'd forget every promise he ever made to himself about taking the relationship slowly. If he could want her the way she looked now, what on earth was he going to do when she was tousled and sleepy across the breakfast table?

Sam backed up another step. "No. Using my house is a bad idea. This scheme will blow up in your face, Clare. Besides, you and I don't have any business cohabiting unless you're willing to risk the repercussions."

Waving off his reasoning, Clare clarified her plan. "We won't be cohabiting. You won't be there. Ellie has to think this is my house."

Miffed at being summarily dismissed, Sam asked sourly, "Where am I supposed to live?"

"The carriage house. You said it had a bedroom. You've stayed there before! Remember, the porch light goes out at midnight."

Sam's back came up hard against the door, and he tried to pinpoint the exact moment he'd lost control of the conversation. "This will never work. She'll figure it out. What about your phone number?"

Wiggling her eyebrows, Clare said, "Call forwarding."

"Unless she's incredibly stupid, she's going to notice the address is wrong."

Clare waved that objection away. "Ellie never sends any of her own mail. She's got a personal assistant for that."

"And she won't be the least bit suspicious about some strange man skulking about in your carriage house?"

"You can play the role of the old-fashioned boarder. You get three squares and a cot. We need to work on the Japanese proposal anyway. Come on, Sam." She gave him a conspiratorial wink. "Where's your sense of adventure? This will be . . . fun. And aren't you the one who's always telling me to have fun?"

Sam counted to ten.

"What could possibly go wrong?" she prodded.

"This," Sam answered, and pulled her against his chest, covering her mouth with his.

Tenderness had no place in this kiss. Sam wanted to show her that playing with fire could burn her. He was tired of her ignoring what simmered between them. Her mouth was hot and smooth as he slid his tongue home. He felt her body tense, relax, and then tense again as his

hands cupped the curve of her bottom. Cradling her between his thighs, he held her close enough to feel the
strength of his arousal before sliding his hands to the
small of her back and beneath the waistband of her pants.
Beneath her panties.

For Clare, shock gave way to the knowledge that she
wanted to feel his hands on her. His touch created a
dangerous throbbing between her legs. The rough texture of his fingers excited her as he leisurely explored the
contours of her hips. His tongue was just as slow explor-
ing her mouth. Vaguely, Clare was aware that the bones
of her legs had melted and that the support of Sam's
embrace was the only thing that kept her upright.

Suddenly, Sam pushed her away and said, "That's
what can go wrong."

The respite from the sensations cascading through
her was so abrupt that Clare felt like a fire blown out
with an explosion. The heat lingered, but the flames were
gone. Every fiber in her body was in an angry uproar at
being awakened and then ignored.

Numbly, she said, "That's why you're staying in the
carriage house."

"You think a few hundred feet will make a difference?
Clare, that kiss wasn't a friendly peck on the cheek. For
either of us."

"I know that!" Clare snapped. "I have been kissed
before."

"If you *borrow* my house, you'll probably be kissed
again."

Clare sucked in a breath at Sam's point-blank warning. If she went through with her plan, she took another
step into a relationship with Sam. He'd make sure of
that. If she didn't borrow his house, Ellie would know

she'd lied, and she'd be poor Clare again. The checks would start coming again.

"This isn't about us. All I want is your house, Sam."

Exasperated, Sam banged the back of his heel against the door. "You want a helluva lot more than you're willing to admit."

"I want the house, Sam. Just the house." She hated to beg, but she needed his house to save face with Ellie. Belatedly, she realized that with his knowledge of the East, he was more likely to understand about saving face than anyone she knew. "Don't make me go back to being poor Clare."

His resolve weakening, Sam cursed beneath his breath and rubbed the back of his neck. Each time he saw her, she cut a little deeper into his heart. Why Clare? She was so wrong for him. She wanted the job security and success that didn't matter to him anymore. She was obsessed with outrunning her childhood. Afraid to lose control.

"Sam." This time Clare's voice was soft, hopeful.

His resistance was draining away like hourglass sand. He didn't want to say no, but yes was an invitation to trouble. Already he'd begun to imagine her in his bed. *Trouble.* Clare might be ready physically to return his passion, but she was a long way from being emotionally and mentally ready to accept more than friendship. He wanted her to lose control, and she wasn't ready. Nor was he prepared to torture himself with thoughts of her in his big four-poster, stretching like a cat, one strap of her gown slipping down a shoulder as she slid from the bed, the soft light streaming in the window revealing every soft, rounded curve—

Think, he told himself. *Think.* He couldn't have Clare

staying at the house. Clare wouldn't thank him for sliding beneath her barriers or the sheets. Not yet anyway.
No, having her at the house would be too dangerous.
She'd tempt him to want to care about security and success again because they were important to her. And that
he couldn't do.

The only sane response was a firm, nonnegotiable no.
But it would also erase all the hope and trust he saw in
her face just then.

Sighing, Sam opened his mouth to refuse when inspi-
ration struck. He didn't have to be the one to say no.
Someone else could do the job for him. "You can borrow
the house. On one condition."

Elated, Clare agreed instantly, "Name it."

Sam schooled his features into a serious mask. "William has to agree. I won't ask him to lie. He makes his
own decisions."

Doubt crept into Clare's voice. "Do you think he'll
agree?"

In a pig's eye, Sam thought to himself before saying,
"Are you sure this is what you want to do, Clare? Tangled webs have a way of snaring the people that weave
them."

"Careless people maybe. Not me."

The kitchen table was half covered in newspapers.
William sat in one of the cane-back chairs, humming and
tapping his foot to an imaginary piece of music. He
hadn't looked up upon their arrival and continued with
the job at hand. Deftly, he snapped the stem and tip from
a green bean and tossed it on the newspaper. A few more
snaps created plump green sections which he tossed into

an enormous old ceramic bowl decorated with faded French roses.

As William reached into the bushel basket beside the chair, Sam cleared his throat. "I need a favor."

The butler snapped the tip from another bean and then fixed Sam with a jaundiced eye. "Why else would you be standing in my kitchen and stubbing your toe on the linoleum as though you were twelve and wanting another cookie?"

"Actually, I'm the one who needs a—" Clare stepped forward to explain, but stopped as she breathed in the pungent green aroma that triggered a sense memory. "God, fresh snap beans. I haven't had those in ages. Not since I was a kid. My uncle loved them." She reached toward the bowl and waited for William's approval.

"Well, hurry it up! And don't paw all of them," he ordered with asperity, but his expression softened the sharp words.

"I used to sneak into the kitchen and help the cook snap them," Clare confessed before she popped the bean into her mouth to relish the crisp, garden-fresh taste.

Asking for a vegetable sample was more than a trip down memory lane. Clare was stalling for time, and she knew it. For some reason, facing William with her dilemma made her feel dishonest. The man's entire demeanor created an image of old-fashioned values: truth, justice, and the American way. Sam might be sure of William's reaction, but she wasn't. What would the stern may say when she asked him to pretend to be *her* butler? Swallowing, she smiled what she hoped was a charming smile and searched for words, wondering how she could have forgotten her carefully planned explanation.

The awkward silence grew as William got up, scraping the wooden chair legs against the floor. Efficiently, he gathered up the newspapers covered with stems and damaged beans and threw the neatly folded bundle in the garbage. When he turned back to Clare, a smile split his lips as if he knew a secret. "It's been a long time since a young lady asked this old man for help. You better stop chewing on the words and ask me quick, so I can say yes before I remember how much trouble favors can be."

Helplessly, Sam listened to the tolerant chuckle in William's voice and realized his mistake. Grinding his teeth produced a grimace, but he managed to hold back the expletive that rose to his lips. He'd been counting on William's ingrained sense of propriety. He'd been counting on William to give Clare a lecture on honesty and facing up to life. But he'd forgotten that his butler had taken a fancy to Clare the first time he met her. He'd forgotten that Clare had a knack for handling the older man. And he sure as hell hadn't expected William to agree before he even heard the request!

"Don't you think you ought to listen to what Clare has to ask before you blindly agree?" Sam asked, unwilling to believe that William would go along with Clare's scam once he understood what would be expected of him.

Bristling visibly, William drew himself to his full height. "Miss Clare is a lady."

"And how would you know?" Exasperation deepened Sam's voice. "You've met her only a few times! For God's sake, William, she wants to borrow the house for the next two weeks and pretend she owns it to impress her supermodel cousin. You're supposed to be her butler, and I'm supposed to be the poor, struggling boarder who rents a room over the carriage house! Are you going to put up with that kind of foolishness?"

William raised an eyebrow, and Clare closed her mouth which had dropped open during the flurry of words. On the wall behind the stove, an old round-face clock ticked loudly into the silence. To Sam, the ticks sounded a lot like accusations—jerk, jerk, jerk, jerk.

Breaking the clock's rhythm, William said, "If I catch our boarder raiding my refrigerator, I expect I'll be laying a baseball bat upside his head."

"You're going to do this!" Sam huffed in disbelief and threw up his hands. The impossible situation he feared had become a reality. "You've both lost your minds. You deserve each other. Now, if you don't object, I'll go pack a few essentials while you and *Ms. McGuire* iron out the details of renting *my* house to her."

After Sam made his ungracious exit, Clare expelled the breath in her lungs in one long whoosh. As she held out her hand, she noted that her handshake was steady at least, even if her emotions were shaky. "Thank you, William. I appreciate this. My reasons are a little more complicated than Sam's explanation."

"Are they now?" William asked with a knowing look, and then tilted his head as he shook her hand. "Doesn't matter."

"You don't mind?"

Chuckling, William dumped his beans into a colander. "Mind? I suspect life is about to get interesting around here. You're going to bother that boy a darn sight more than name tags in his shorts."

Clare leaned against the counter and hugged her midriff with her arms. "It'll only be for a couple of weeks. Maybe less. And you'll like Ellie. Everyone does."

"Do they now?"

"Always. You'll see when you meet her tomorrow."

"Tomorrow!" William fairly shouted the words as he dropped the colander in the double sink. "Child, why didn't you say so sooner!

"Tomorrow," William mumbled, unrolled his sleeves, and reached for a gray Windbreaker that hung on a peg beside the back door. "Lord. Company's coming tomorrow and nothing but leftovers in my refrigerator."

"But—" Clare began, trying to slow William down before he stormed out the door.

"But nothing. I'd best get to the store. If Rebecca gets here to cook in the morning and finds out we're expecting company and there's no food in the house—" William shuddered. "Well . . . she'll be mad as a cat in an alley full of hound dogs."

The slam of the door reverberated through the kitchen, and in a few moments Clare heard the sound of a car engine. Finally, the ticking pulse of the old clock replaced the noise of William's departure and reminded Clare that she was alone in the house with Sam. Nervously, she poked her head into the dining room, half expecting to see Sam striding toward her, ready to change his mind about the house regardless of William's approval.

When he didn't materialize, she wandered through the rest of the downstairs, wincing at the occasional squeak of her tennis shoes on the hardwood floor. Skulking about the house and waiting for Sam made her feel uncomfortable. Guilty. *Dammit!* If Sam hadn't wanted her there, why hadn't he simply said so instead of relying on William to do his dirty work? If he wasn't happy, it was his own fault. She refused to feel guilty because his little plot failed. With a deep breath to fortify her courage, she climbed the staircase.

Only one door along the upstairs hallway was closed. Tapping lightly, Clare waited for permission to enter. When none came, she called, "Sam?"

"What?" The question was sharp, even cross in tone.

Resting her forehead against the door facing, Clare plunged ahead. "We need to talk."

Suddenly the door swung wide, and as she jumped back, Sam filled the opening. "I don't want to talk. I said you could borrow the house if William approved. He did. You can. Now, do you mind if I finish changing clothes?"

"N . . . no," Clare managed to say, and forced herself to calmly face the half-naked man in front of her. Sam's chest and feet were bare. The cut-up jeans hung precariously on his hips and the open button above the zipper formed a provocative V that drew her eyes downward. Her mouth and throat went dry at the sight of dark bronze hair disappearing into the V. Swallowing gave her something to do and eased the dryness in her throat.

"I'll wait out here," she said more primly than she intended. Unable to stop herself, she looked down the hallway, wishing the cavalry hadn't just ridden off to the store.

Sam stepped back and leaned a forearm on the door edge. "I'm only changing shirt and shoes. If you think you can handle it, you can come in."

"Of course I can handle it," Clare said stiffly. "I was attempting to be polite. However, if I'd known you were an exhibitionist, I wouldn't have bothered."

As Sam pulled her into the room, his eyes glittered

dangerously. "Not an exhibitionist, Clare. Voyeur maybe. At least, where you're concerned."

Clare froze as the door clicked softly into place, and Sam stood silently behind her.

"You see," he continued, leaning so his voice was close to her ear, "I don't want to show off. I want to watch you hover on the edge and fall off the world with me."

The thud of her heartbeat sounded in her ears, and her lungs fought to continue the subconscious act of simply breathing in and out. "Stop it, Sam. You're going to make the situation impossible for both of us."

"It's already impossible for me," he whispered into the soft skin at the back of her neck, his nose almost brushing against the nape. "I need you, and you're completely wrong for me. You don't want what I want. You don't care about fun."

"Sam—" Desperation invaded her voice. He hadn't so much as laid a finger on her, and her knees were already beginning to buckle.

"Just say *no*." He repeated the popular slogan not as advice to her, but as if he were pondering the power of those three little words. "So simple. But I didn't. And now you're here. Punishing my imagination. Of course, I'm not the only one who'll be tortured."

He adjusted his body to fit the curves of her bottom, pressing his bare chest against her back and holding her lightly by the shoulders. His words feathered the lobe of her ear as he spoke. "Look around. You're in my bedroom. This is where you'll stay because you don't want to explain to Ellie why you haven't taken the master bedroom.

"You're going to sleep in my bed because your pride

won't let you admit I get to you. That would be the first step in losing control, and you can't do that. You don't want people in your life who'll endanger your safe, comfortable routine. You don't want magic or surprises. That's why you'll tell yourself that sleeping in my bed won't make the slightest difference."

As he spoke, her gaze shifted to the wide four-poster, exactly as Sam had intended. Her imagination supplied images of tangled sheets and entwined limbs. Clare's eyes widened as she realized that regardless of whether or not the bed was stripped and the sheets changed, it would smell like Sam. Going to sleep would be like immersing herself in his scent, wrapping herself in his essence. This was *his* room. All around her.

"I've never made love in that bed," Sam said, his hands beginning to massage her shoulders.

Closing her eyes against the onslaught of feeling, Clare knew she was losing the battle for control. Sam's slow hands erased the tension in her shoulders. She swayed backward, letting his strength support her for a moment before she angrily pulled away to put distance between them.

"Don't do this, Tucker. It's not fair."

"Fair?" Sam's eyes narrowed. "I never promised you fair."

"You promised friendship," she accused him as she turned around.

"And you used it to get what you wanted—this house for show-and-tell with Ellie."

Then Clare sucked in a breath, and Sam ruthlessly quelled the impulse to apologize or drop his gaze. What he'd said was the truth. Whether she liked it or not. He wanted more than sex from Clare. He wanted a little self-realization. She had to see that the pattern of her life would eventually leave her empty and alone. She didn't want people to care about her, and he had to find out why.

Clare's chin snapped up as she said, "I didn't use you. I offered to pay you for the house. I'm going to pay you. This is a business deal."

"This isn't about money, Clare. This is you hiding from your past. Which is why you're never going to have a future." Sam turned away from her before she could answer and walked to his closet. He swept several neatly hung shirts aside, considering and discarding them without conscious thought.

"And who the hell are you to make that assumption about my future?" Clare demanded when she could finally speak.

Sam pulled a white polo shirt off the hanger and turned. "Who am I? You don't want to know, Clare. When you know a person's secrets, good or bad, you can't ignore your feelings anymore. The secrets are always there in your mind, something you share with that other person. Creating a bond. You still want to know who I am, Clare?"

She put out a hand to steady herself against the long mahogany bureau littered with bits of Sam's life: loose change, cuff links gathering dust, school photos of towheaded young boys, and an open paperback mystery. She nodded and said, "I want to know how you can stand there and presume to tell me I have no future. I've worked damned hard for five years to get what I want and where I want."

Tossing the shirt onto the bed, Sam crossed the room until he stood in front of her. "Because I learned the hard way that the people in your life, people you love, are all that matters. When I spent all my time and energy avoiding chaos and unpleasantness, I also avoided the joy in life. When I spent my days worrying over budgets and meetings, I didn't have any time left for my widowed father or the woman in my life."

He paused, making sure he had her complete attention. "Because while I was busy being busy, my father committed suicide when the loneliness in his life became unbearable."

Stunned, Clare felt the pain of his confession wash over her. Guilt over a parent's death was something she understood. Instinctively, she reached out.

Sam caught her hand before her fingers touched his bare chest. "I changed my life, and I won't go back to schedules and profit margins, Clare."

"Who asked you to?" Clare whispered, nervously aware that Sam's gaze shifted from her eyes to her mouth and that he hadn't let go of her hand.

"You did." Sam inched closer, never taking his eyes from her mouth, making her a promise. "I want more than you can give, and if you stay here, you're going to have to learn that people and family are more important than a tidy life."

"I don't think so."

"No?" Sam whispered the question against her lips and then drew back a fraction, waiting.

Clare couldn't answer without opening her mouth to the heat of his. Ironically, that's exactly what she wanted to do, and the impulse scared her. For the umpteenth time, she asked herself: *Why him? Why not him?* came the uneasy reply. She wasn't a virgin. An adequate affair in college had opened her eyes to the mysteries of the sexes. She knew exactly what he wanted.

So why was she suddenly dismayed by the prospect of kissing him? Because this wasn't college, and she instinctively knew that Sam was a great deal more than adequate. She closed her eyes, only to see his strong hands in her imagination as they slid over her body. A moan of frustration escaped her. Her body wanted something her mind knew would be a mistake. Body and soul overpowered logic as she leaned forward.

SIX

Sam let her come to him, but the wait was unbearable. Seconds felt like minutes. Finally, he heard the soft sigh of surrender, and her lips met his. His body responded hard and fast to the feel of her fingers as they brushed across his nipples.

He tried to fit her body to the length of his, and growled angrily when the bureau didn't provide the support he wanted. He needed to feel every inch of Clare against every inch of himself. He needed a wall or a bed. He had both. Clare gasped when he scooped her up, but his mouth on hers silenced any protest she might have made. Depositing her on the bed, he followed, letting a leg rest between her thighs and his arousal press into her belly.

The slow, sensual movements of his body against hers made Clare conscious of the pulse of desire that arched her back and began her own rhythmic movements against his thigh. At the motion, Sam made a sound that was unmistakably satisfied as he pulled her shirt off her shoulder far enough to trace her collarbone with his tongue.

The trail blazed by his mouth and tongue was hot, wet, and then cold as he moved on to the skin above her breasts. Clare luxuriated in the forgotten feelings of being held and touched. Desired and aroused. Of losing control. Her fingers craved the texture of his skin, the ripple of muscle beneath her touch.

Impatiently, Sam unbuttoned her shirt, pushing aside the fabric. Clare caught her breath as Sam paused, tantalizing her with promises as his forefinger dipped beneath the lace edge of her bra to tease her nipple. When he flicked the hardened nub, Clare bit her tongue to hold back a moan. The pulse between her legs began to escalate to a throb. Conscious choice ceased to exist. The dance began in earnest.

"Sam—" The ragged sound was warning, plea, and satisfied sigh.

"Shh," Sam whispered against her neck. He kissed her lips, her eyes, and the shell of her ear as he began to strip her. A lazy smile tugged at his mouth as he felt her kick off her shoes. The shirt was disposed of quickly enough, but he lingered over the bra. The dark rose of her areolas was visible through the sheer lace. Each nipple jutted upward, straining the cloth. Slowly, he fingered the front clasp, sliding his hand over the creamy mounds before releasing the catch.

"Samuel!" William's voice was faint, but without a doubt drawing closer. "Miss Clare!"

The words dashed ice water on Clare, and she struggled free of Sam's intoxicating hold. All she could say as she grabbed frantically for clothing was "Oh, my God. Oh, my God."

Sam's language was more colorful and varied.

"Samuel?" William tapped on the door, and Clare disappeared over the side of the bed despite Sam's attempts to stop her.

Cursing again and snatching up the white polo shirt, Sam managed to look unruffled as the door swung wide. He tossed the shirt over his head and mumbled, "Yeah?"

William knitted his brow and looked curiously around the room. "Where's Miss Clare?"

Sam shrugged his shoulders into his shirt. "Don't know. Isn't she downstairs?"

"Now, would I be asking you if she were?"

"She's probably gone over to the carriage house," Sam offered, purposely nonchalant.

"You don't say?" William didn't say anything more, but he stared with great interest at a spot on the floor beside the bed. Sam's eyes closed briefly as he remembered the soft thud of Clare's tennis shoes as they hit the Oriental rug. Recovering his composure, he knew better than to look down. Being caught wasn't the same as admitting he was caught. And he had no intention of telling Clare, who crouched out of sight, that William had spotted her shoes.

"What do you want, William?" Sam tried to keep his voice even.

"Money. I got to the store before I realized I was going to have to stock the whole kitchen."

Sam frowned and tucked in his shirt. "The household emergency fund is two *hundred* dollars, William. That buys a lot of food. We're having one guest, not the Queen of England and her entourage!"

The butler raised his eyebrow, a subtle reminder that sarcasm wasn't necessary. "Samuel, I don't care if you stock the kitchen or not, but don't ask me to explain to Rebecca *why* we have company coming and no food."

"She's your daughter!"

"That's why I won't be doing the explaining."

Since Rebecca's tongue was every bit as sharp as William's, Sam fished his wallet out of his pocket and silently handed several twenties to the older man. William's eyes widened, once again riveted to the spot on the carpet that boasted Clare's sneakers. Risking a glance from the corner of his eye, Sam watched as a feminine hand carefully pulled the last tennis shoe beneath the bed.

William nobly ignored the mysteriously disappearing shoes. "When you see Miss Clare, you tell her not to worry. I'm going to treat her right."

"When I see her, I will tell her," Sam agreed darkly, and jerked his head toward the door.

"I'm going now," William said a little too loudly.

"Not soon enough," Sam muttered under his breath, knowing that by then Clare had convinced herself yet again that losing control was her worst enemy. She'd never laugh about this fiasco, never see the humor in the situation.

William ambled toward the door and stopped halfway there. "I expect I'll be gone for quite a while this time, what with buying the food and all."

"Fine," Sam gritted out between clenched teeth as he advanced on his butler with every intention of shoving him bodily out the door if necessary. Obviously spurred onward by the look in Sam's face, William crossed the threshold a fraction of a second before the door banged shut behind him.

"Samuel." Even through solid oak the older man's voice was loud and strong.

Sam hung his head in defeat and pulled open the door a crack. *"What!"*

"I think we'll put Miss Clare's guest down at the end of the hall. In Pamela's old room. That way the noise on the stairs at night won't disturb her."

"Whatever," Sam agreed, and slammed the door again before William's subtle observation registered in his consciousness. *That way the noise on the stairs at night won't disturb her.* The impact of those words sent fear into Sam's heart. William approved. William was matchmaking. Unraveling the threads that kept Clare wrapped tighter than a drum was going to be hard enough without William lending a hand.

"Is he gone?" The disembodied words floated toward him from beyond the bed.

"For the moment. But William's like flypaper. Once he has a hold on you, he's very hard to get rid of."

Clare peered over the bed and swept the room with her gaze. Apparently satisfied, she plopped her shoes on the bed and elbowed her way to a standing position. Sam noted the shirt he'd worked so hard to remove was now securely buttoned and hugging the curves he should have been hugging. The thought irritated him as much as Clare's nervous posture did.

"Thank heavens I remembered the shoes," she said, gesturing lamely toward them. "You don't think he saw them, do you?"

"No," Sam lied. "Come here, Clare."

She actually took a step toward him before sanity rescued her, pushed the panic button, and reminded her how close she'd come to losing control before. The man leaning so casually against the door represented everything she struggled to eliminate in her existence. He didn't care about control. He wanted anything and everything in life. He encouraged her *to want, to lose control.* And she couldn't do that. She couldn't. Bad things always happened to people who lost control.

The first time she could remember completely losing control, she'd told the people she loved most in the world to go away and never come back. And afterward, wanting her parents back had hurt too much. Wanting to be loved like Ellie was loved had hurt too much. Wanting to be anyone but poor Clare had hurt too much. When she finally stopped wanting and finally got control of her emotions, she stopped hurting. A hard lesson, but one she learned very well. A lesson she didn't want to learn again.

No was a hard word to say to Sam, but she said it.

"Dammit, Clare. We're adults. And contrary to what my butler thinks, this is my house. What we do to and for each other is none of William's business. I intend to straighten that out first thing tomorrow."

Startled, Clare said, "William has nothing to do with this."

"Then come here," coaxed Sam.

"No." The refusal came easier this time, especially since she didn't look in his direction.

"Hey," Sam said softly as he pushed away from the door. "Look at me, McGuire. I'm not suggesting a quick tumble in the sheets and money for cab fare. I never have been very good at one-night stands."

Clare lifted her chin and drilled him with as honest a gaze as she could muster. "Too bad. I'm not much good at anything else."

Looking as if she'd just landed a solid blow to his midsection, Sam dropped the hand reaching for her back to his side. She circled the bed and sat down to put on her shoes. "I need to get home and pack. I'd better make a list. I've got a million details to settle before tomorrow. Not the least of which is figuring out where everything is in this house. Ellie will never believe I live here if I don't know where the silverware is."

As he watched the efficient, list-making perfectionist sneak back into Clare's personality, Sam managed to contain his anger. Barely. He'd never wanted to shake a woman in his life until then. But he wanted to shake Clare, shake some sense into her, make a connection. The minute he got close, she pulled in her emotions like a turtle pulled in its head and shut the flap. Why did she need the wall around her?

A better question would be why did he care? Why had he continued to push inside her defenses? Why hadn't he gone looking for the right kind of woman to love? One that would have been capable of loving him back? Sam felt the blood drain from his face as he confronted the one fact he'd overlooked. He was falling in love with the woman who sat on the bed, knee to chin, tying her shoelace.

Spending two weeks with Clare had given him glimpses of the woman inside the tidy package—the woman vulnerable enough to trigger his protective instincts, sexy enough to plague his dreams, and complex enough to fascinate him. Not to mention clever enough to involve him in her scheme to fool Ellie. His neat little plan to settle down with a comfortable woman had fallen apart the moment Clare crossed her legs and challenged him to prove he could teach her anything. The hell of it was, if he didn't teach her to want people in her life, he'd lose her. If he couldn't teach her to lose control, and fast, he was in for a lot of hard, lonely nights. *Patience*, he told himself. He needed patience.

"The everyday silverware is to the right of the sink," he said as she tightened the last bow. "Company silver is in the butler's pantry. But William will handle the table setting if you have dinner guests."

Clare laughed suddenly. "Guests? Practically everyone I know will be under this roof. Whom would I invite?"

"Your boarder, of course." Sam grinned and tried to convince himself that he could outlast Clare's demons.

After wrestling a large suitcase onto Sam's bed, Clare began to unpack. While she had made the trip to the condo to pick up her cat and her clothes, William had efficiently emptied the mahogany bureau. The clothes of Sam's closet not moved to the carriage house had been relocated to an unused guest room, and Clare had no doubt that William had already changed the sheets.

William's attention to detail had stripped the room of any physical reminders of Sam. So why did Sam's presence still fill the room, pressing against her? Because when she'd arrived, Sam gave her one of those heart-stopping looks before deserting her in favor of the carriage house. That look had been both a threat and a promise. William, on the other hand, had been nothing but gracious, as though her stay would give him nothing but pleasure.

Clare groaned, realizing that Sam's behavior sent the exact same message but with a completely different affect on her nerves. Methodically, Clare transferred her clothes to the bureau and sternly told herself to forget him. Sam's room was nothing more than a hotel room. The only difference was that Sam probably didn't have stationery and a Bible in the nightstand drawer. She reached for the drawer handle and pulled, not really expecting anything, but irresistibly curious. What she found made her suck in her breath and sit down on the bed.

Why would a man who hadn't made love in this room have condoms in the nightstand? And why should she be shocked? Or care? Either William had overlooked a few personal items, or Sam was making a subtle point.

Clare picked up one of the foil packets and knew William hadn't forgotten anything. Sam had slipped them into the drawer. She had to close her eyes against the rush of sensation that spilled through her body. This was Sam's way of telling her that he was impulsive but not reckless. His way of telling her that he wouldn't ignore the chemistry between them and that she'd better be ready.

Heat seeped into her bones as she fought the memory of his thigh riding high between her legs as she arched and rubbed against him. Throwing the packet back into the drawer, Clare slammed it shut and paced the room. Good Lord, what was she going to do? He wouldn't give up, and he wasn't the kind of man who'd settle for pure and simple sex. If there was such a thing as pure and simple sex! At least not with Sam. Not the way he put his hands on her and turned the world upside down.

"*Meow.*"

Slick broke her train of thought as he leapt up onto the bed and fell over, rubbing his head along the pillows. Clare stared at him and envied his ability to make himself at home so easily. *No, don't you dare envy that damn cat!*

she cautioned herself. *You've got no business relaxing right now.* This was Sam's house; she was only trespassing. So no relaxing. No ties. No emotional involvement. What she didn't have, she couldn't lose.

She believed in safe. She believed in secure. No risk. No hurt. Sam believed in rolling the dice and taking the chance. Not her. No sir.

By the time she'd finished unpacking, she had control of her emotions, and the clock read almost midnight. Every muscle in her body ached from the tension of fending off Sam. Her shoulders were impossibly knotted. Her head throbbed, and her conscience pinched her for planning an elaborate charade to fool Ellie. Wearily, she ran water in the old-fashioned claw-foot tub in the adjoining bathroom and then added foaming bath oil. After a day like today, she needed a good, long soak with no distractions. Returning to the bedroom, she pulled her white gown out from under her contented cat, who'd curled up on it the minute she laid it out, and grabbed her cosmetic bag.

"Clare?" Sam called from the hallway and knocked on the door. "I saw the light from the carriage house. It's late. Anything wrong?"

Stunned, Clare glanced at the clock again and then at the window. Sam could see her room—*his room*—from the carriage house. He'd been watching? Crossing the room, Clare threw the gown over her shoulder and opened the door a crack. Sam leaned against the door facing, his shirt unbuttoned as though he'd thrown it on at the last minute. While his chest wasn't completely bared, she could see the definition of his pectorals and the flat stomach that disappeared into the low-slung jeans. *Half-dressed. Hurriedly dressed.*

"I'm fine," Clare managed to say, and dragged her gaze to his face. She'd never known a man more casually masculine than Sam. "Thank you for asking."

As Sam listened to her polite conversation, disappointment nagged at him. He'd expected to find Clare ready for bed, and to be painfully honest, he'd hoped to find her soft and drowsy, not fully dressed and wary. "Mind if I come in?"

"Yes."

"Suspicion does not become you, Clare."

"I have reason to be suspicious."

A grin appeared on Sam's face. "You have good reason to be suspicious. However, right now I need my toothbrush. William is efficient but not perfect."

"Oh." Clare blushed, pulled her gown off her shoulder, and stepped back. "I'll get it."

Sam pushed opened the door and caught her around the waist as she turned. "Don't bother. I know the way."

"Oh," Clare repeated as his hand slipped away, and she watched him disappear into the large bathroom. Dimly, her mind registered the fact that he was barefoot. She told herself that's why he moved so confidently. That explanation was better than comparing him to a predator who'd cornered his quarry. And knew it.

Retrieving his toothbrush should have taken only a second, but Sam lingered. A black silk robe with neon-pink flamingos lay carelessly across the closed toilet seat. His tub churned with the unfamiliar sight of iridescent bubbles, and the heat of the water sent an incredible fragrance of hot spiced apples into the air. Knowing that Clare would soon be naked and submerged in the perfumed water gave Sam ideas that would keep him up all night. Regretfully, he turned off the running water which had pushed the shimmering bubbles almost to the edge of the tub.

As he reached for his toothbrush, he saw one of his shirts hanging on the back of the door. The toothbrush he took; the shirt he left. And he grinned at himself in the mirror. That old shirt was about to become very important.

"Got it," Sam said, gently waving the toothbrush as he reentered the bedroom and found Clare still standing by the door, nervously clutching her white gown. He crossed the room and stopped in front of her. As always, when he looked down at Clare, he became fascinated by the shape of her lips and the deep blue of her eyes. Everything about her turned him on. He wanted to feel the weight of her breasts in his hands again. He wanted to hear her sigh his name as he entered her.

His voice was raspy when he said, "I turned off your water."

"Thanks." The word sounded as though it had been scraped across her vocal cords, and Clare wished she could ignore the hunger in Sam's eyes. But she couldn't. She parted her lips and leaned a fraction of an inch closer, willing him to kiss her, willing him to end the suspense, willing him to make the decision she couldn't make.

" 'Night, sweet Clare. Your water's getting cold," he whispered, and left her, an odd smile on his lips.

" 'Night, Tucker," Clare echoed, purposely using his last name to regain some distance from the emotions that pulled at her every time Sam walked into a room.

As the door clicked shut behind him, Clare crumpled her gown into a ball and tossed it on the bed. Sexual frustration was a new and unfamiliar sensation for her.

Angry, she began to strip, throwing her shoes across the room to the closet before she realized that Sam had accomplished exactly what he wanted. She was losing control. The temper she'd held in check for years was beginning to slip away from her more often. She'd yelled at Dave that morning, Sam that night, and now she was throwing shoes.

"No," Clare said as she flipped off the overhead light and headed for the bath. "I won't let him get to me. I like my life. I am not changing. Not even for him."

A sigh escaped her as she slid into the hot water and leaned her head against the tub's rolled edge, which felt as if it were made to support her neck. "A few days and this will all be over," she promised herself. She could go back to her normal routine, and Sam could go back to creating chaos in someone else's life.

Why did that idea bother her so much?

Sam sat on the top step of the staircase, whistling softly and waiting. Five minutes should be enough time for Clare to undress and sink into the bubble bath. Just five more minutes, and he'd have her right where he wanted her. Again. He could have kissed her when he said good night. She'd wanted him to kiss her, but she'd also wanted him to hurry up and get it over with.

He grinned at the thought of his kiss being as anticipated as cherry-flavored cough syrup—necessary medicine with a taste that was *not exactly* horrible. From any other woman the attitude would have been insulting, but in Clare the attitude signaled progress. Grudging progress, but progress nonetheless.

Consulting his watch, Sam pushed himself up and

walked back down the hall to his door. He knocked once, loud enough to be heard in the bedroom, but not nearly loud enough to be heard in the bathroom. Any twinge of guilt he felt at his devious actions was ignored. All was fair in love and war, and Sam knew his relationship with Clare was definitely one or the other. He just wasn't sure which.

When he didn't hear an answer to his knock, he eased open the door and called her name softly, hoping he wouldn't get a response. He didn't. The room was dark, but a shaft of light spilled through the partially open bathroom door. An unfamiliar pink flamingo night light glowed beneath the bedside table, drawing his attention. Practical Clare either had a weakness for flamingos, or she was afraid of the dark. Considering the robe he'd seen earlier, he had to believe she liked flamingos.

Slick hopped off the bed and wove himself between Sam's ankles, purring loudly. Sam grinned, placed a finger across his lips as though the cat were a co-conspirator, and continued to the bathroom.

"Clare?" he said softly as he rapped on the door with one knuckle. "Are you decent?"

A gasp and the sound of sloshing water answered his question. Neither of them said anything for a moment, and then Clare said in a strained voice, "I'm taking a bath."

Grinning, Sam said, "Good. Then you're decent. I saw the bubbles earlier." When Sam pushed open the door and found Clare reaching for a towel, he stopped her with a gesture. "No, don't get up. I won't be long."

Clare snatched her hand back and drew her arms across her breasts, which were barely concealed by the foam, and sank deeper into the water. A blush flamed her cheeks, and anger flashed at him from her eyes. *God, she was gorgeous.* Sam felt his manhood jump as a sudden pulse of desire ripped through him.

"Go away," she ordered calmly, but the ragged rhythm of her breathing suggested she was anything but calm.

"I expected that."

"Then why did you come in?" She pressed her lips together and tilted her head, waiting for an explanation, silently telling him that the explanation had better be a good one.

"I'm missing a shirt, and I thought it might be in here." Sam made a pretext of looking behind the door and feigned surprise. "Ah, here it is."

"And that couldn't wait until tomorrow?" Clare snapped.

"Probably." Sam tossed the shirt into the hamper and scooped up her flamingo-covered robe from the toilet seat before making himself comfortable. "But *I* couldn't wait until tomorrow."

Clare gasped, her control and her dignity hanging by the same thin, frayed thread. The world suddenly closed in around her, narrowing to exclude everything except Sam Tucker and his incredible brown eyes, which seared her with every gaze and advertised his hunger. Although she tried, she couldn't look away. Absurdly, she felt like a satellite trapped in a disintegrating orbit headed for destruction. The heat of her body suddenly made the water feel cold, causing her nipples to harden and pebble beneath her hands.

"You've got nowhere to hide, Clare. You can't evade

me or my questions unless you leave the room. To do that, you're going to have to stand up, and I warned you once before"—Sam paused for emphasis—"I like watching. What's it going to be, Clare? Conversation or my heart's desire?"

His question sucked the oxygen from the air, leaving Clare breathless. How could he sit there as though they were across the breakfast table and admit that he wanted to watch her rise naked from the bath so he could look at her? A shiver ran up her spine as she wondered what it would be like to have Sam watch her, enjoy her. He made her feel strange and wild, and for a moment she almost stood up. Almost. Then sanity returned, and her brain began to work.

"William wouldn't approve of this."

Sam threw back his head and laughed. "You have no idea exactly how much William does approve. He even tolerates your cat."

"What does that have to do with anything?" Worried by the steady disappearance of her frothy white shield, Clare gathered more of the concealing foam around her and drew her knees up so that the only parts of her body exposed were her shoulders and kneecaps. "I want only the house, Sam. You can't just walk in on me anytime you feel like it! We had a deal."

"Not anymore. And I warned you that a few hundred feet wouldn't keep you safe." Sam let the silken material of the robe he held flow through his fingers. "Besides, I didn't walk in. I knocked. You didn't answer."

"That doesn't give you the right to wander into my bath and settle in like you belonged here, like you were invited. Dammit, Tucker. There's an invisible line that a gentleman doesn't cross."

"I crossed *that* line this afternoon, Clare."

Memories invaded Clare's consciousness, and she closed her eyes against the longing that shot through her body. She could still feel every touch, hear every word he had breathed against her skin. With an effort she pushed the longing away and simply looked at Sam, afraid to trust her voice with any reply.

"Great robe," Sam whispered huskily as he rubbed it against his chest. His eyes closed briefly, and then he looked at her, considering her as his hand trailed the silk across his flat belly. "I'll bet it feels even better with you in it."

Sam didn't bother to disguise his passion. He devoured her with his gaze. For a heart-stopping moment she was afraid he was going to lean over and touch her. And then she was afraid that she was going to beg him to slide his hand beneath the water and caress her. Below the disappearing foam, she fisted her hands and fought for control.

"Sam, I don't want you here," she forced out.

"Liar. You want me every bit as much as I want you. The only difference is you refuse to admit that you need anyone—for anything."

Clare's chin came up as he knew it would.

"Get out of my head, Sam."

"Then tell me why you run like a scared rabbit every time I show you that I want you."

She stiffened, and shifted her knees back to beneath the water, covering herself with her arms. "I don't run away."

"Yes, you do, sweet Clare. Why don't you have people in your life?" Sam asked softly, wondering if she knew just how much he wanted to be a part of her life.

"I'm not in your class anymore. I don't have to answer."

"Okay. I'll try an easy one. Who's your best friend?"

Clare's eyes dipped to stare at the white foam, but she didn't answer.

"Come on," Sam encouraged. "Who knows more of your secrets than anyone?"

When Clare looked at him, sadness turned up the corners of her mouth, making the smile bittersweet. "You. You know more of my secrets than anyone. Happy now? You've gotten another confession out of me. Will you go?"

Instead of making Sam happy, her answer twisted unpleasantly in his gut. He pitched the robe over the hamper and dropped to his knees on the rug beside the tub, heedless of the dampness and cold of the porcelain against his belly. Without giving her a chance to pull away, he captured her face with his hands.

"What are you afraid of, Clare? That I'll find out too much? What do you keep buried inside you?" For a moment he searched her eyes, trying to find the answers he wanted from her, wondering why he needed answers. "If I keep looking, what will I find, Clare?"

"Nothing you'll like," she whispered.

"You'd be surprised by what I like," Sam told her as he eased his hands down her neck, massaging her shoulders with his fingertips. As he drew her up and forward, the scent of apples made him hungry for a taste of her, as did the feel of her water-softened skin and the slippery texture created by the foaming oil. "Perfect women bore me, Clare."

"Then I must be driving you crazy," she said unsteadily.

"That's one word for it," he rasped, and let go of her shoulders before he forgot that he had no business seducing her in the middle of the night. Patience, he reminded himself. Firmly, he pushed himself to a standing position, ignoring the fact that bath foam no longer covered the creamy skin of her breasts. "The first night we met, you asked me if I ever had an impulse I didn't act on. Remember what I said?"

"Yes."

"Good. I'm going to let an impulse fade away right now. I'm not going to do what I want to do, but you think about it. Think about what I'm not going to do." He reached for the brass handle of the door. "Anticipation and foreplay. Helluva combination. Good night, Clare," Sam said softly, and left the bathroom.

When the bedroom door clicked quietly shut, Clare remembered to breathe.

"Please, check again," Clare said desperately, then paused and bit her lip. She tried to block the mental image of Ellie catching a cab and showing up at the condominium. Continuing more calmly, Clare explained, "Ellie, my cousin, wasn't on the early flight this morning. She's got to be on this one."

"I'm sorry," said the flight attendant, sounding genuinely apologetic. "But I'm certain all the passengers are off. Maybe you looked away as she left the plane. Why don't you try the baggage claim area?"

"Thank you. Maybe I will." Clare gave the woman a weak smile and walked away, wondering why disaster had followed her like a black cloud for the past few months.

Before she'd taken more than a few steps, Clare

stopped, finally admitting that rushing off to baggage claim would be a foolish waste of time. She'd gotten to the terminal gate a full thirty minutes before the plane landed. She'd studied the faces of every man, woman, and child as they'd gotten off the plane. She'd watched joyous reunion after joyous reunion. Her attention hadn't wandered, and Ellie wasn't on the plane or in baggage claim. After everything she'd done to make the visit perfect, Ellie hadn't even bothered to show up.

At the moment the long walk through the terminal and out to her car required more energy than she had. Feeling defeated, Clare leaned against the cool wall and stared at the empty blue plastic chairs and deserted boarding counter of Gate 47. She couldn't even begin to think about what to do next. Everything in her life had been put on hold, waiting for Ellie's arrival.

Adrenaline had gotten her through the day, through the hours of tedious reading and research about the Japanese auto industry, through the endless mountain of paperwork on her desk. Adrenaline had pushed her along from task to task, making her forget the dread that had settled in the pit of her stomach as she waited for the Saturday evening flight. Adrenaline had persuaded her that Ellie would actually believe she belonged in Sam's house.

Sam's house. Sam's bed. Sam. Those were thoughts that had kept her up all night when she should have been worrying about how to handle Ellie. Instead, she'd lain in bed, replaying the scene in the bathroom over and over, trying to discover why the thought of Sam rubbing her robe against his stomach escalated the unfamiliar rush of blood in her veins. She'd struggled with how to handle him and the sensuous thoughts he skillfully deposited in her imagination.

The man planted erotic images and nurtured them like a master gardener. She'd never met a man who occupied her thoughts the way Sam did. Even when he wasn't with her, she couldn't keep him out of her mind. She heard his voice in her dreams.

"Pensive? Clare McGuire in a pensive mood?" Sam was suddenly flesh and blood beside her, grinning at her as he teased, "What are you doing, Clare? Compiling another list? Am I on this one too? Or at least on your mind?"

Startled, Clare pushed away from the wall and evaded his hand. She refused to let him brush her cheek which burned with guilty knowledge. Sam Tucker had most definitely been on her mind. "What . . . what are you doing here?"

"I came to find you." Sam deftly captured her shoulders and brought her to him for a chaste peck on the lips. "I missed you today."

"Why?" Clare asked, and pushed him away as heat suffused her bones and threatened to melt her reserve.

"That is a particularly stupid question," Sam informed her before taking her hand in his and answering, "I missed you because I like having you around."

Clare stared at her hand nestled in his and realized that she had no intention of pulling away from the comfort his touch offered. When she looked up into Sam's face, she said, "You came looking for me because you missed me?"

"No," Sam said gently as he started down the corridor. "I came looking for you because Ellie called to say she's been delayed."

Lose Yourself In 4 Steamy Romances and *Embrace A World Of Passion — Risk Free*

Here's An Offer To Get Passionate About:

Treat yourself to 4 new, breathtaking romances free for 15 days. If you enjoy the heart-pounding and sultry tales of true love, keep them and pay only our low introductory price of $1.99*.

That's a savings of $12.00 (85%) off the cover prices.

Then, should you fall in love with Loveswept and want more passion and romance, you can look forward to 4 more Loveswept novels arriving in your mail, about once a month. These dreamy, passionate romance novels are hot off the presses, and from time to time will even include special edition Loveswept titles at no extra charge.

Your No-Risk Guarantee

Your free preview of 4 Loveswept novels does not obligate you in any way. If yo decide you don't want the book simply return them and owe nothir There's no obligation to purchase, yo may cancel at any time.

If you continue receivi Loveswept novels, all future shi ments come with a 15-day ris free preview guarantee. If yo decide to keep the books, pay on our low regular price of $2.66 p book*. That's a <u>savings of 24</u> off the current cover price $3.50. Again, you are nev obligated to buy any books. Yo may cancel at any time b writing "cancel" across ou invoice and returning th shipment at our expens

Try Before You Buy

Send no money now. Pa just $1.99* after you'v had a chance to read an enjoy all four books fo 15 days risk-free!

*Plus shipping & handlin
sales tax in New Yor
and GST in Canad

Save
85% Off The
Cover Price on 4
Loveswept Romances

Get 7 Loveswept Romances

For The **Low Introductory Price**

Of Just $**1.99***

*Plus shipping & handling, sales tax in New York, and GST Canada.

Titles receive differ those sh here w the l Lovesw selecti

No Risk. No obligation to purchase. No commitment.

"Delayed?" Clare echoed. Then her eyes snapped wide open and she gasped, "Oh, my God, you didn't answer the phone, did you?"

"Sorry," Sam confessed, his eyes narrowing as he noted that Clare's first reaction hadn't been concern over Ellie's delay. "I pick up the telephone when it rings. I know it's a bad habit. I'm trying to stop. Really I am."

"This isn't a joke, Sam." Unconsciously, she rubbed her thumb against his and gripped his hand more tightly. "You really did talk to Ellie?"

"Don't worry. She doesn't suspect a thing. I told her I was the gardener."

Clare almost stumbled and stared at Sam, knowing he couldn't possibly have read her thoughts earlier. Nevertheless, she wondered why he'd chosen a gardener instead of a painter or electrician. He always seemed to be one step ahead of her, reading her mind, analyzing her.

"Something wrong?" Sam asked.

"Everything," she said, irritated. She sighed and pulled her hand away from his. "Now I've got a butler, a boarder, and a gardener to explain. Why couldn't you have let the machine take a message as we agreed?"

"Because I never expected Ellie to be on the other end of the line. By the way, does she always talk in that melodramatic, breathless way?"

Clare's eyebrows drew together as she stepped on the escalator that would take them down into the parking garage. Ellie's voice had been described as earthy and sensual, but never melodramatic and breathless. "You don't like her voice?"

"Not particularly." Sam stepped onto the escalator behind Clare, placing his arms on either side of her.

He found it interesting that they were talking about everything except Ellie's delay and when she'd be coming, but he didn't mind. For the first time since he'd met her, Clare wasn't thinking about Ellie's arrival or Ellie's approval. She was thinking about *his* approval of Ellie, and if he read her right, she was comparing herself to her cousin again, wondering whose voice he liked better.

"As a matter of fact, I don't like her voice at all," he corrected her, and leaned down to breathe in the scent of her hair. He let his tongue lightly touch the side of her neck before he whispered, "Your voice, however, I definitely like. The faint drawl is sexy as hell. Find a dark corner, and I'll show you just how sexy."

"Oh, for heaven's sake," Clare said as she caught herself leaning back into Sam's chest. Straightening, she scrambled down the escalator.

"You're running, Clare."

"Damn right!" she agreed, stepping on the solid concrete. No sense in denying the obvious anymore. She had a bad case of raging hormones. "Running as far and as fast as I can until Ellie decides to show up. I can't think with you touching me all the time." She stopped, suddenly struck by a thought. "When *is* Ellie coming?"

"She's not sure. Maybe not for a week."

"A week!"

"Yeah, what a shame," Sam said, pretending sympathy for her disappointment and taking the opportunity to drape an arm around her shoulders and walk with her. "But you don't have to move back to the condominium. I'm a man of my word. I said you could use the house until the crisis with Ellie passed."

A whole week alone with Sam? She'd be crazy to tempt fate. Already, she'd become accustomed to his habit of touching her, of absently pulling her close as though she belonged at his side. Just yesterday her temper had gotten the best of her twice. She couldn't afford to live in Sam's house. He was the kind of man that was habit forming, and she didn't want to have to live through the withdrawal pains when he moved on.

Because he would move on. She was a challenge to be met, mastered, and ultimately forgotten. She had no doubts that he would forget her. After all, her aunt and uncle had taught her how easily "poor Clare" could be forgotten. No, she shouldn't tempt fate. She had to keep him at a distance, away from her heart. Away from her body. Especially away from her body. Because he had no intention of ignoring the chemistry between them.

"I'd have to be a fool to stay in your house, Tucker," she said sweetly, disguising all the turmoil beneath her calm exterior. She dug in her purse for her car keys. "And I'm not a fool."

Confused, Sam asked, "Now, exactly what is that supposed to mean?"

Clare rolled her eyes and a disbelieving huff escaped her. "Two plus two *plus* the condoms you put in the nightstand drawer add up to trouble."

"Condoms!" Sam exploded, and then quickly glanced at the rows of cars beside them, groaning as his gaze met that of an interested nun. Shrugging his shoulders, he nodded an apology and turned away. He planted both feet firmly beneath him and swung Clare around to face him. Very carefully, very slowly, he asked, "What condoms?"

SEVEN

Clare could feel the tension in Sam flow down his arms and through his hands into her body, flowing until it filled her, stretching her taut. His dark eyes held hers and demanded an answer. Suddenly Clare felt as though she stood in quicksand, and every word out of her mouth threatened to sink her deeper into the quagmire. Shrugging off his hands, Clare separated her car door key from the others on the ring.

"Forget I said anything," she suggested as she turned toward the pale blue Spitfire convertible. She had no intention of having a conversation about—of having *this* conversation with Sam. What on earth had possessed her to bring up the subject of condoms?

"What condoms, Clare?"

The softness of his repeated question didn't fool her. Sam wasn't going to let the matter drop quietly into the black hole of misguided conversations. Not Sam. Sam didn't like secrets. He'd dig and pry, just like he always did, until he was satisfied with her response.

"Don't play innocent with me, Sam Tucker," she finally answered, and glared at him. "You know as well as I do that I'm talking about the condoms I found in my—*in your*—nightstand."

"I didn't put any condoms in *our* nightstand," Sam said as he pulled her completely around to face him. He slid his hand slowly down her bare arm until he cupped her elbow. "I didn't have condoms in the nightstand, because I've never made love in that bed."

"Right! Well, if they don't belong to me, and you didn't put them there, then who—" Clare stopped abruptly, and her mouth hung open for a second before she snapped it shut.

William!

Jumping to the same conclusion a fraction of a second before Clare, Sam said, "I'll kill him."

"You can't kill family." Clare's tone implied regret.

"Watch me," Sam invited her.

Clare's face burned as she thought of William tactfully placing the condoms in the drawer. To hide her embarrassment, she focused on unlocking the car with shaky hands, her keys making a faint tinkling sound.

"He saw my shoes on the rug," she whispered as Sam's hand steadied hers.

Sighing because he understood exactly what she was referring to, Sam drew her away from her struggle with the door lock and forced her to look up at him. Distressed eyes met his, and he hated the misery he saw there. Hated that her own passion embarrassed her and wondered if he could ever make her realize that love and loving weren't to be hidden in a closet, but to be shown off in public and shouted from the rooftops. Like his parents had.

"Shh, Clare," Sam soothed as he fit her body against the length of his. "What if William did see the shoes?"

"What *if* he did?" Clare repeated as though she couldn't believe her ears. When she'd extricated herself from Sam's embrace, she threw a brief glance around the parking garage and lowered her voice. "Your butler knows we've—thinks we've—he saw—"

While she struggled to find the right words to describe their activities, Sam raked his hands through his hair. Slowly, he let his hands trail over his neck and down his jawline, but he restrained the impulse to shake Clare and to provide her with a vocabulary of blunt, explicit words to describe what they'd almost done. With every fiber in his being he ached to tell her, *in plain English*, everything he'd like to do to her, for her, and in her. Most of which would probably shock the hell out of her sense of propriety. All of which would certainly disturb William a lot more than her shoes on the rug.

Unexpectedly, a deep chuckle rumbled through Sam as he remembered what he'd said to Clare while she was in the bath the previous night. *You have no idea how much William approves of you.*

Mistaking his chuckle for amusement at her, Clare clamped her mouth shut and pulled open the door. With a thump her purse landed in the passenger seat, but Sam caught her arm before she could disappear inside the convertible. "Hey, come back here. I wasn't laughing at you. I was laughing at William's paternal instincts. I'm thirty-three years old, and he still thinks it's his job to keep the big bad wolf from the family door."

"And why is that funny?"

"This time around," Sam explained with a wry grin as he pinned her lower body against the small car. A satisfied growl escaped him as the distance between them evaporated, bringing her full breasts in contact with his chest. "This time around, you're the family, and I'm the big bad wolf."

"You're the . . ." Clare's sentence trailed away when his hips moved in a circular motion that pressed his arousal against her. She sucked in a tiny breath and said the first thing that came to mind. "My, what big . . . *eyes* you have."

"All the better to see you with, my dear," Sam whispered, sinking his fingers into her hair and wishing he could do more than that. Tilting her head, he let his teeth gently scrape and pull her bottom lip. "Open your mouth, Clare," he ordered. "Let the wolf in."

The flicker of need that hovered in her belly whenever Sam came near her flared into full awareness. He smelled like autumn sunshine, and she wanted to bask in the warmth for once without worrying how long it would last, without regard to the consequences. She was tired of being careful and tired of being disappointed, tired of controlling the impulses nurtured by the image of Sam and her damned silk robe.

Hesitantly, Clare let her hands creep up the cotton knit shirt and curled her fingers into his collar. Would one kiss be that crazy? Just one kiss. A barn-burner to teach Sam the dangers of playing with fire. One kiss to cleanse her system of the awful anticipation he'd created last night by leaving her alone with her fantasies. One kiss on her terms, with her in control. With confidence Clare pulled Sam closer and opened her mouth.

Barn-burner was as apt a description as any for the searing kiss that scorched her logic and melted her fantasies. Heat invaded her mouth as Sam slid his tongue against hers. With his hands still cupping her head, he controlled her movements, taking pleasure from her mouth and giving it back to her. This became Sam's kiss, not hers. He stoked the fire, and she burned.

"Let's go home, Clare," Sam suggested as he pulled his mouth from hers and rested his forehead against hers. "I will not make love to you in a parking garage! Besides, your convertible is too small. Why in God's name couldn't you have a nice, practical minivan with tinted windows instead of a tiny thirty-year-old convertible?"

"The Spitfire will double my investment in five years," Clare answered unsteadily, painfully aware she'd been passionately kissing Sam in a public place. Her lips still throbbed from the pressure of his, and her head throbbed with the knowledge that a few moments earlier she would have gladly traded the convertible for the minivan. So much for teaching Sam a lesson. So much for staying in Sam's house. She'd simply have to find some other way to deal with Ellie.

"I'm not going home with you, Sam. I have my own car. But I am going there to pack. Please," Clare whispered as she pushed at Sam's chest. "People are staring."

Sam let her go. "Let them stare. And separate cars or not, you are going home with me. I'm not going to spend the next week packing and unpacking every time Ellie gets the urge to plan a trip and you need a house."

"Well, I'm not going home with you," Clare repeated as she slid into her seat and unrolled her window. "Because I'm not spending the next week worrying about when and where you're going to strike next."

Sam's laughter rang out, echoing through the concrete garage and drawing the attention of several passersby. "If you're worrying about sex, Clare," Sam cautioned in a smooth drawl, "you are worrying about the wrong thing! Never waste brain cells worrying about the inevitable."

The engine roared to life, and Clare threw the gearshift into reverse. "I'm not worried about the inevitable. I'm worried about how I'll like prison life when I'm found guilty of murdering you."

"If I don't bring you home, you won't have to worry about prison. William will murder me first. He's the one who sent me after you. He thinks you need us."

"I'm not staying, Sam." Clare backed out of the parking place and roared away.

Sam grinned as the powder-blue sports car sped off. Softly, to her taillights, he said, "You go right back to my house and pack up if you think that's best, but I'd bet the farm that William's going to change your mind about staying. He fixed snap beans for dinner, Miss Clare."

Clare's mouth began to water the minute she opened the front door. With every breath she inhaled the taste of spicy, southern fried chicken, fresh biscuits, and vegetables. She could hear the clatter of pot lids in the kitchen and William's strong baritone singing. She wondered what it would be like to really live in this house, to come home to an interfering butler and home-cooked meals every day. To know that someone waited for her, cared about her.

Startled by the direction her thoughts had taken, Clare put a straitjacket on her imagination and headed for Sam's room as quietly as possible. Packing—not daydreaming—should be her number-one priority. She needed to get her clothes, her cat, and get out. Tonight. Before anything else disastrous happened.

But first she needed her suitcases, which were nowhere to be found. They weren't under the bed. They weren't in the closet. They weren't under the guest beds or in the guest room closets. Her suitcases seemed to have grown feet and run away from home. Seeing no other choice, she went downstairs to ask William where he'd moved them.

As she entered the kitchen, she found him lifting out the last piece of golden-fried chicken and turning off the stove. The kitchen door was open, and the screen door let the sweet scent of spring steal inside the house. William's song had been replaced by whistling, and the generic vegetable smells sorted themselves into the specific aromas of snap beans and squash.

"William," Clare said softly, and tried to erase the image of the man putting condoms in the nightstand.

A broad smile creased William's face as he turned. "Ah, Miss Clare. I guess Samuel's already gotten ahold of you."

Shock lowered Clare's bottom jaw for a moment, until she realized William wasn't making a comment about the progress of her intimate relationship with Sam. He referred to Sam's airport mercy mission. Clare managed a shaky smile, wishing William hadn't put those condoms in her drawer. Now everything he said was tinged with double meaning.

"Yes. He told me about Ellie and the delay. I'm really sorry to have put you to all this trouble for nothing."

William chuckled. "No trouble. Food's got to be fixed whether you're here or not. Whether we have company or not. You just go on in to supper. I was about to come and fetch you anyway."

"Oh, no!" Clare said, eager to make him understand about her plans. "I can't stay for supper. It's so late, and now that Ellie's not coming, I've got to get packed and out of your way. That's why I came downstairs. I can't find my suitcases."

William allowed himself a disapproving grunt. "Don't know why you want to run off now. Your suitcases will wait. My chicken won't."

"He ought to know," commented Sam, who miraculously appeared in the room as though from thin air. "Fried chicken is his specialty. Rebecca does most of the cooking—casseroles, lasagna, soup—but William can cut up a mean chicken. He could teach the Colonel a thing or two about special recipes."

Clare started to make another excuse about packing, but stopped as she noticed how William's chest puffed up at Sam's praise. If she refused to taste his chicken, he'd be insulted and disappointed. Suddenly she discovered that she didn't want to repay William's many kindnesses with rudeness. He deserved better.

Grinning broadly at Clare's dilemma, Sam continued. "He won't even let anyone near his kitchen when he's frying up some of the South's finest. He's afraid they'll learn his secret—a tiny bit of Cajun heat in the batter."

Gently, Sam propelled her toward the swinging door that led to the dining room. "Eat now. Pack later. William cooked a mess of snap beans. You wouldn't want to hurt his feelings after he's gone to this much trouble, would you?"

Well and truly trapped, Clare pressed her lips together and shot Sam a withering stare. He'd known she'd cave in and stay for dinner because he'd known all about William's little cooking spree while they were at the airport. That explained his cocky attitude. He'd had an ace up his sleeve, and she'd been outmaneuvered by the master once again. But that didn't mean she was down for the count. No matter how hard he tried, Sam wasn't going to cajole or guilt-trip her into staying.

But for William's sake, she'd postpone her packing until after dinner.

Unfortunately, *after* dinner was a long time coming. William seemed to have lost the spring in his step. He brought out the food dishes one at a time, placed them very carefully on the table, and shuffled slowly back to the kitchen for the next item. He conveniently forgot to put ice in their tea glasses, which necessitated another delay as he returned to the kitchen for ice.

And Sam made no effort to dig into the meal, preferring, instead, to wait until William finished setting out the entire meal. Finally, dinner was served, and Clare wasted no time in devouring her portion. Neither she nor Sam bothered with conversation.

"Mmmm. The chicken was wonderful." Clare licked her lips and tossed her napkin on the table.

"How could you tell?" Sam drawled. "You didn't even chew before you swallowed."

Guiltily, Clare noted his meal was less than half finished. She'd inhaled her food in the hope of excusing herself to pack. In defense of her table manners, she said, "I was hungry."

Sam didn't bother to call her a liar. He contented himself with raising one eyebrow and tilting his head. "Then I'm sure you can't wait for dessert."

"Dessert?" Clare echoed and looked at her watch. "Nine o'clock is too late for dessert. I've got to pack. Then, when I get home, I've got reading to do on the Japanese deal."

Sam set his tea glass down with more force than necessary. "First Ellie's coming and all you can do is clean. Now Ellie's *not coming* and all you can do is pack. Can we stop dealing with Ellie and your job long enough to deal with us?"

"Us?"

"Us—you and me." Sam swung an index finger between them. "One plus one equals two. What's wrong? Is this a new concept for you?"

Right on cue, the kitchen door swung wide. William brought in strawberry shortcake and pretended not to notice the fog of tension in the air as he removed their dishes and beat a strategic retreat through the kitchen door.

"Damn," Sam uttered, briefly closed his eyes, and shook his head at the interruption. "Look, Clare, forget the cake. We need to talk." He pitched his napkin beside hers and rounded the table. He pulled her to her feet and jerked his head toward the front of the house to indicate they were moving. In answer to her unspoken question, he said, "Someplace other than within earshot of William."

Loud cleaning-up noises suddenly emanated from the kitchen.

"See what I mean?" Sam asked. "Little kitchens have big ears."

Clare pulled away from him, shaking her arm slightly to dispel the sensual imprint of his touch. "No matter where we have this conversation, talking isn't going to change my mind."

"Then you have nothing to fear, do you? Ladies first," Sam ordered, and stepped aside.

Sam followed her to the living room, and while she settled into the corner of the couch, he paced. Pacing was the only way he could control his impulse to touch her. For some insane reason, Clare always looked like she needed a hug. Reaching for her was becoming a habit.

"Think about this situation from the logical perspective, Clare. You and I need to work together on Dave's Far East deal. If you stay here, we'll save a lot of time. You've already moved in. I've already moved out."

"We won't be spending that much time working together." Clare studied her nails and smiled as Sam's pacing took him past the arm of the couch and behind her. "All you need to do is review my proposal, make suggestions, and coach me on a few points of etiquette. How long could that possibly take?"

"Considering how well you listen? A long time."

Clare started to take offense until she realized that Sam's purpose was to draw her into a worthless argument and keep her arguing until it was too late to leave that night. Sidestepping his ambush, she said, "Then I'll pay more attention when you talk. Is that all?"

"Not quite." Once again Sam's pacing brought him into her line of vision and then out of it as he offered his next point of reasoning. "If you stay, William can finally earn his salary instead of spending his days twiddling his thumbs."

"You couldn't care less whether he earns his salary. He's family."

"It will make him feel useful, keep him busy, and that's important at his age."

Clare didn't even bother to turn around when she answered. If Sam wanted to make her uncomfortable by carrying on this conversation with the back of her head, then fine. "William looks in good shape for his age. I don't think you have to worry."

"No, but you do. Ellie will eventually arrive." Sam's voice was soft, seductive, as if he were sure he'd played the winning card. "You need this house."

Not as much as I'm beginning to need you. Clare pushed away the idea, not ready to admit that somehow in the last few weeks she'd gone from being happily single to unhappily alone. She'd lost the ability to keep herself separate from Sam. She knew that leaving his house was the only way she'd ever put Sam back into a little box marked "interesting and nothing more."

Somehow he'd become important, and she hated that. She didn't want anyone to be important in her heart. She didn't want to lose anyone else. Not feeling at all was better than the pain that always came from losing.

First she'd lost her parents, and then she'd lost hope that her aunt and uncle would ever love her as they loved Ellie. One by one the servants who'd patched her skinned knees and helped her with her homework either retired or simply left her aunt's house for other employment. As a child, she hadn't understood that the help was paid to bandage her scrapes and guide her through tricky math problems. She'd foolishly thought they cared about her. And when they left without good-byes, she felt abandoned and hated it.

Over the years she'd grown very good at keeping busy so she couldn't feel. Staying in Sam's house meant opening up her emotions again. If that was the price she'd have to pay for staying, she had no intention of paying it.

Quietly Sam leaned over, kissed the top of her head, and said, "And God knows why, but I need you."

Then he left her alone with her conscience.

The suitcases had miraculously appeared in her room. Only now Clare didn't care. She didn't feel like packing. She felt like crying. She hadn't cried in years, and she had no idea what she wanted to cry about now. But she recognized the sensations, the burning in her eyes, the lump in her throat, and the crumbling of her self-control.

Sam Tucker scared her. She wanted to stay in his house and come home to laughter. Carefully, Clare positioned herself at the edge of the window and stared at the carriage house. *I need you*, he said. Not *I want you*. Just *I need you*. Unusual choice of words.

Any other woman would jump his bones and be done with it. So what was wrong with her? Why couldn't she take the chance? Why couldn't she be more like Ellie? Why couldn't she see the cup as half full instead of half empty?

Because she was alone. Her closest relative was a cat named Slick. When life didn't work out, she couldn't pick up the phone and call her parents for advice. She couldn't wire "Pop" for money when the budget got tight. If her heart got broken, no one would be there to pick up the pieces.

Suddenly Clare couldn't bear the thought of going back to her empty apartment that night. The next day would be soon enough. Besides, ten o'clock was too late to go anywhere, she reasoned. She shoved the suitcases off the bed and told herself that staying the night wasn't weakness, but common sense.

By the time Clare showered and crawled into bed, she'd convinced herself that she'd be up and packed by the crack of dawn. Gone before anyone noticed she'd spent the night. Gone before she had a chance to change her mind again.

She patted the bed and called to Slick. When he didn't jump up onto the comforter, Clare scooted to the edge and hung her head over to look beneath the bed. "Psst, Slick. Get up here, you lazy cat. I need a hug tonight."

Slick wasn't under the bed.

Rolling her eyes, she got out of bed and crossed to the closet. Slick had a passion for dark corners and high-heeled shoes. Opening the door, Clare ordered, "Stop hiding in there and come to bed."

When Slick didn't come out, she flipped on the ceiling light and called him again. Puzzled, Clare opened the hall door and said his name, expecting him to bound out of a guest room. He didn't.

"Where is that darned cat?" Clare whispered, unease beginning to blossom in the back of her mind, but she refused to consider any of the dark possibilities her subconscious offered. Finding Slick was simply a matter of going downstairs, and when she found him, she'd give him an earful about wandering off at bedtime.

She returned to her room and pulled on her robe, not bothering with the sash. Instead, she wrapped it across her chest and held it in place with one arm. Slick was a fairly intelligent cat—when he wasn't chasing feathers and swinging from curtains. All the same, she'd feel better if she knew he was asleep at the foot of her bed instead of clawing up Tucker's family antiques or getting into mischief. Quietly, she tiptoed downstairs and whispered his name.

Each dark room greeted her with silence and nudged her uneasiness toward panic. By the time she reached the kitchen, all she could think about was the open kitchen door and William cooking at the stove earlier, the screen door letting the breeze in.

"He hates the outside," she told herself as she stared at the wooden door that was now safely closed and locked for the night. "William wouldn't have let him out. I made sure to tell him that Slick was a house cat. He wouldn't have let him out. Slick's not gone. He is not gone!" she repeated more firmly.

Then where is he?

Her breaths were too short to supply enough oxygen to her lungs. A tear slipped out of the corner of her eye. Slick might be a pain in the rump, but he was her pain in the rump. He was all she had. She refused to believe he was outside in the dark, scared, and in a strange neighborhood.

Just to be sure, she'd open the door and call him. Even though she knew he wasn't outside. Yes, just to be safe, she'd call him. Clare pulled open the door and her heart sank. "Oh, my God."

The old screen door had a tear in the bottom panel. A hole large enough for a determined cat to get through. Clare's lip began to tremble as she sucked in and expelled air in rapid succession. Each breath became more ragged than the last.

"Oh, Slick. You don't even know what a car is."

Clare banished the image from her mind and pulled herself together. She had to think clearly. How long could he have been gone? Two, maybe three hours. Not long. *Long enough*, her panic whispered. He can't have gone far, she argued silently. *Far enough*, came the grim response.

Resolutely, Clare stepped outside and called Slick. The cat's name fell from her lips and sank into the still night air like a heavy pebble into water. The word created ripples in the silence, but the ripples didn't reach far enough because the quiet enveloped her again.

Please answer me, Slick, she prayed silently as she waited.

Sounds of the night answered her, but not her cat. Acceptance made Clare's heart thud in a sickening rhythm against her chest as she turned instinctively toward the carriage house. Her cat was gone. She needed help. She needed a friend. She needed Sam.

Clutching her robe, she ran across grass wet from a brief shower and barely noticed the dampness. Nor did she feel the coolness of the brick walkway beneath her bare feet. Her only thoughts were that together, she and Sam could find Slick. They could work out a plan.

Light still shone through the windows and curtains of the ivy-covered-brick carriage house, but Clare wouldn't have hesitated even if the windows had been dark. She banged on the door and waited only a split second before calling, "Sam. Sam!"

Impatient, Clare tried the door, and when the knob turned, she breathed a thank-you and let herself in. "Sam, I need—"

Clare skidded to a halt after taking only two steps into the room. Sam looked startled but comfortable, his feet propped up on his desk. Slick lay draped across Sam's lap, doing his boneless cat imitation and looking contented and safe.

"Need what?" Sam asked cautiously, swinging his feet off the desk. A masculine sixth sense straightened Sam's spine and tensed every muscle in his body. The night had opened up his door and thrown a whirlwind into the room. Or so it had seemed to him when Clare burst through his door, flamingos swirling and chest heaving. She was breathless and breathtaking. She was dressed for bed, which meant she'd decided to stay, but something was terribly wrong.

"Who the hell do you think you are?" Clare asked, relief and anger making her voice shake. The flood of relief only made her realize how frightened she'd been, how scared she still was, and how alone she'd be if anything happened to Slick. "How could you? You think this is some kind of game where you push my buttons and I dance to your tune?"

Sam tossed his paperback mystery onto the desk, gathered Slick up from his lap, and stood to face her. He chose his words carefully, uncertain of what he'd done. "Slow down, Clare. What are you talking about? What do you need?"

"I need what's mine!" Clare shouted at him, knowing that her emotions were out of control, but she was beyond caring. One hand strangled the doorknob, and the other curled into a fist. Sam had no right to take her cat, to make her think she'd lost Slick. Slamming the door released some of her tension, but not all. Not nearly all. She needed her cat. Clare crossed the room and pulled Slick out of Sam's arms.

For a minute she buried her face in fur, rubbing her cheek against the softness, letting the reality of his small, warm body invade her senses. Unconsciously, she cradled Slick in her arms and rocked him gently back and forth. *It's okay. He's back. He never left.* Bit by bit, the fear began to subside. When she looked up at Sam, she had her emotions under control. "Don't ever do that to me again. Don't ever take my cat."

The words were calm, but raw emotion, barely held in check, stared at Sam from her eyes. A faint moisture trail still glistened on one cheek, and she clutched Slick as though she'd never let go again. Without warning, the last piece of Clare's puzzle slipped into place in Sam's mind.

Dear God, he realized, she loves that cat, and she's terrified of losing what she loves. She lives her life according to schedules and rules because that gives her control. And if she's in control, losing is a decision she makes and not a quirk of fate. She doesn't trust the world to open a new door for every one it closes.

Knowing that, he understood her terror when she burst into the carriage house, and he understood her genuine anger because she thought he'd taken her cat. He wanted to gather her up and make the fear go away, but he didn't. Touching Clare while she was vulnerable was too much like taking advantage of her, like offering a starving child food.

Gently, as if he were afraid to upset her, Sam said, "William asked me to take Slick. He was in the way in the kitchen when he was trying to clean up."

Clare's eyes widened. "*William* asked *you* to take *my* cat away?"

"Slick was making a pest of himself." Sam smiled. "Cats and garbage cans don't mix. Especially when chicken bones are involved. Since I didn't mind the company, I took him with me. William promised he'd tell you." Sam traced the fading path of the tear on her cheek until she pulled away. "I'm sorry, Clare. We didn't mean to frighten you."

"I wasn't frightened!" Lifting her chin, Clare tried to ignore the blood that had begun to race through her veins at the realization he was barefoot and bare-chested. Even to her ears she sounded out of breath as she said, "W-worried, of course, but not frightened."

"Right." Sam raised a brow and raked her from head to toe with his eyes, lingering at her breasts. "You always run around barefoot, wearing next to nothing and breaking down doors?"

Clare groaned something inarticulate, shifted Slick, and pulled her robe closed over her gown. Right now she didn't really remember what gown she'd put on. Not that it mattered. Since she liked pale silks, any of her gowns were sheer enough to be embarrassing. She had no doubt that this one revealed details of her anatomy that were better left concealed.

"No, I do not normally run around breaking down doors, but then, I'm not usually subjected to the practical jokes of southern gentlemen and their butlers."

Sam advanced toward her. "Clare, I would never intentionally frighten you. And neither would William." Once again he flicked his gaze over her. This time he smiled. "Since you obviously weren't planning to leave us, he didn't see the need to tell you."

"But I *am* leaving." Clare backed toward the door,

wishing now that she hadn't slammed it in anger. "To-morrow."

"Why didn't you go tonight?" Sam asked. "Why wait?"

Slick made an unhappy noise and began to struggle against her tight grip. Clare calmed him, uncomfortably aware that she'd run out of room. Her back touched the door. As Sam closed the distance between them, she was reminded that when he walked barefoot, Sam moved like a predatory animal closing in.

Without a shirt, Sam lost the civilized veneer. He truly became the wolf at the door, and she found herself wanting to invite him in, to let him devour her, to be lost in the rush of feeling.

Another step, and he'd be so close, only light could pass between them. Another step, and it would be too late. Too much had happened that day; she couldn't trust her instincts. So Clare whirled and reached for the knob.

Sam's palm shoved the door closed again almost before she'd opened it. "Why did you wait, Clare?"

As she tried to decide on an answer, Slick wiggled free and hit the floor with a thud. Without him she felt defenseless, deserted, under siege. "It was late."

"Why did you wait, Clare?" Sam repeated as his other hand flattened against the wall, framing her body between his arms.

Sam surrounded her from behind, invaded her space, made her knees weak, and he hadn't even touched her. He did all this to her and still wanted her to think clearly enough to answer questions. She couldn't. Each movement magnified the tiny rustle of silk against silk and brought to mind the image of Sam with the robe cascading through his fingers.

"Why did you wait, Clare?" Leaning into her, Sam aligned his body with hers, letting the flamingo robe tease his chest with memories. "Tell me," he whispered, wanting her to admit she needed them. "Why didn't you leave?"

EIGHT

"I was lonely." Clare rested her head against the door. "I didn't want to go home to the quiet and the dark."

Sam closed his eyes against the swift rush of satisfaction that swept through him. *Halfway. She'd come halfway.* He hadn't realized the hole in his life was so big until he'd decided he wanted Clare to fill it. The muscles in his abdomen tightened as he waited. He wanted her to acknowledge what had been building between them. She had to want to make love as much as he did.

"That's not true. Not completely," she said, and braced her hands, palms flat, against the door. "What have you done to me, Sam? Why do I keep thinking about the way you touch me? I don't want to feel this way. I don't want to be lonely."

Sam smiled. *Close enough.* He pulled aside the collar of her robe and feathered the back of her neck with kisses as he promised, "Sweet Clare, I can make the lonely go away. At least for tonight."

Slowly, he pulled the robe down her shoulders and tossed it aside, exposing creamy skin and the thin white straps of her gown. She started to turn in his arms, but he stopped her by circling her waist and pulling her hips into the cradle of his thighs. "We'll do this my way."

Clare closed her eyes and leaned back into the strength of his chest. "Maybe we shouldn't do this at all."

"Wrong. We should have done this a long time ago."

Sam slid his hands across her belly and downward to explore contours of her body, the rise created by her hipbones, the edge of her panties, and the swell of her womanhood. Although she tensed and laid her hands against his forearms, she didn't stop him. Sam gently pressed his lips to her shoulder and began to gather the gown with his fingers, reeling in the silk fabric, inch by inch. He felt as though he were unveiling a work of art he had waited a long time to possess.

When the hem of the gown reached her waist, Sam let one hand sample the warmth of her skin and glide over the lace that edged her panties. Her belly quivered beneath his touch, and he marveled at the perfect fit of her body. His tongue teased the shell of her ear as his hand pressed her more snugly against his arousal. He wanted her to feel his desire, to know how hard he was for her.

Clare concentrated on breathing and controlling the shudder that threatened to shimmy through her. Sam's hands were magic. With gentle pressure between her thighs, he let her know he wanted her to open for him. Instinctively, Clare adjusted her legs. When he cupped her, letting his fingers slide into the narrow space between her legs, she gasped and arched her back. To be held so intimately was ecstasy. To be separated from the touch of his hand by a scrap of fabric was torture.

With deliberate care, he drew his hand away, his fingers stroking the sensitive valley. The feeling of loss Clare experienced was quickly replaced by the unexpected sensation of having her breasts bared to the cool air as Sam pushed up her gown and found the aroused buds of her nipples with thumb and forefingers. Impatiently, she tugged the gown over her head and flung it away.

Now nothing separated her bare back from the taut muscles of Sam's chest. Each time he caressed her nipples, he pulled desire through her abdomen and sent need snaking through her limbs. Clare wet her lips as she looked down at his hands, so strong and tan against her pale skin.

Sam stilled the motion of his fingers and tested the weight of one breast in his hands, letting the soft flesh mold itself to the shape of his curved palm. "So soft," he whispered. "So right. God, Clare. Do you know how crazy you could make a man?"

Finally, he turned her in his arms and brought her to his chest. He savored the electric charge that washed over him as flesh met flesh. This is how he'd dreamed of Clare, soft and pliant in his arms. He wanted all of her.

He felt a pulsing need to be inside her, a part of her. But he couldn't satisfy the hunger yet. The fire in his gut was too strong to control. Taking Clare too quickly would be a mistake. He had to wait until the explosion of desire that ripped through his body had settled into a slow burn. Just the thought of burying himself inside her almost took him over the edge.

Sam let out his breath in a rush. "Open your mouth, Clare. Let the wolf in."

When she did, his tongue swept inside, taking what he wanted. With one hand he cupped the back of her neck. With the other he unbuttoned his jeans and slid down the zipper. Sam groaned against her mouth when she helped him by shoving his jeans open. Suddenly the need to have her touch him was as great as his need to touch and be inside her. When her hand closed around him, and slid downward, Sam sucked in some air and adjusted his stance.

His response to her touch gave Clare the courage to satisfy her curiosity about the feel of his body. The masculine contradiction of velvet and steel fascinated her. The muscles beneath her fingers pulsed with life and jumped as she smoothed her palms up his belly and over his nipples which, judging by the swift tightening of his fingers on the back of her neck, had hardened into nubs as sensitive as hers.

Pulling his mouth from hers, Sam studied her, memorizing her face and rubbing his thumb along the line of her jaw. "I don't know which I like more. Me touching you or you touching me."

Clare slid her arms around his waist and leaned into his chest. Very quietly, she said, "You touching me."

Caught off guard, Sam asked, "What?"

"Which I like better."

Her words were like a match to kindling, and in their own way erotic. Sam enfolded her in his arms for a moment before swinging her off her feet bride-fashion and carrying her to the spiral staircase. When he let her down at the bottom step, his voice was unmistakably husky. "I'm going to do a hell of a lot more than touch you."

Once again Sam had become the predator. Clare backed up the narrow, winding stairs as he followed, purpose and desire showing in every step he took. Not once did his eyes waver from her face, but she felt as if his gaze raked every inch of her body. When she topped the final stair, she could feel the heat from the flush of excitement that colored her cheeks and breasts.

"Don't," Sam ordered as she covered her chest with her arms. He stepped up onto the landing with her and pulled her hands away, replacing them with his own, which cupped and pushed her breasts gently upward so he could admire them. He took each areola into his mouth and swirled his tongue across the pebble-hard peaks before he said, "You're beautiful. Don't cover yourself."

Standing quietly and watching Sam touch her was almost more than Clare could take. She'd never felt such a surge of erotic energy and power. Nor had she ever had such little control of her body. Her breasts seemed to swell and push themselves into his palms, begging him to sample her flesh again. An incessant pulse had begun between her legs.

Worst of all, Clare knew she liked Sam's penchant for watching her, looking at her, studying her. She liked knowing she fascinated him.

Sam led her to the edge of the double bed that dominated the spartan bedroom alcove. "Last chance to run from the wolf, Clare. If you don't, I am going to make love to you. And there won't be a thing you or William can do about it."

While he waited, he pulled her toward him, making sure they were belly to belly. Searching his face, Clare found promises in his eyes, dark promises, bright promises, promises that made the ache between her legs worsen. He had wrapped her in desire so tightly, she knew she'd never undo the knot unless she finished what they'd started.

"Make love to me, Sam."

"Yes, ma'am." He said the words against her mouth, but instead of kissing her, he let his lips trail down her neck, between the valley of her breasts, and then knelt to continue his exploration down the center of her abdomen.

When Sam flicked his tongue into her belly button and whisked down her lace panties, Clare felt her heart skip a beat. He'd invaded her space again by holding her thighs apart and gently forcing her back onto the bed. Suddenly Sam abandoned his slow, deliberate seduction and kissed the springy curls at the apex of her thighs, making Clare gasp as his tongue touched her intimately.

She felt as though everything around her—colors, sounds, textures—were suddenly more intense. Sam's touch made the world come to life. Within her own body she felt the stirrings of something so intense, she held her breath against the feeling.

"No." Her reaction was the result of some self-preservation instinct, some inner knowledge that she was reaching the point of no return, a place where she wouldn't be able to hold back any part of herself from Sam.

Knowing that she wasn't ready for complete intimacy, Sam contented himself with one last brush of his lips against her sweetness and stood back up, swiftly ridding himself of his jeans.

Clare shivered. Every inch of her skin was suddenly sensitive. When Sam stripped, she discovered that he wasn't wearing his infamous boxers. She remembered the way the jeans hugged his body and the feel of his arousal pressed against her buttocks. As she watched him retrieve a foil packet from between the mattress and box spring, she realized he'd been expecting her. He'd known before she'd known herself. Somehow that knowledge left her feeling dizzy, as if she were losing her grip on the world.

"You were waiting for me tonight," she said before she could stop herself.

"No." Sam leaned one knee on the bed and stared down at her. "Hoping for you."

The mattress was old and slightly sunken in the middle, which suited Sam perfectly, because Clare fell neatly into his arms the moment his weight joined hers on the bed. Once again her hands found his chest. Her fingers roamed over muscle as if she were soaking up the heat of his body. "Tell me you're sure, Clare. I feel like I'm going to come apart right now if I can't slip inside you, feel you around me."

He pulled her beneath him and pushed the tip of his manhood into the wet softness he found between her legs. "Tell me, Clare."

She answered him by closing her eyes, lifting her hips, and taking more of him.

"God, Clare," he rasped, and sank into her. "You feel so good. Look at me," he whispered. "I want to watch you fall off the world."

Slowly Clare drew in a deep breath and opened her eyes. Just looking at him tilted her world and squeezed her heart. Emotions she wasn't prepared to deal with were there in his eyes, unspoken and dangerous. She knew what he wanted from her, and she wasn't prepared for total surrender, wordless intimacy.

Dear God, was this what he meant when he asked if she was sure? That she'd have to let herself splinter into a thou-

sand pieces at his touch? Every sensation was too much, too quick. Every stroke of Sam's shaft brought her closer to the edge, and she fought the climax building inside her, tensing against the onslaught.

"Don't, Clare," Sam ordered, and groaned sharply at the quicksilver touch of pleasure that shot through him as she tightened. "Don't tense. I can't hold—Clare!"

She felt the fulfillment shudder through Sam as he buried himself deep inside her. Even now her body threatened to spill satisfaction through her, and if that happened, she'd never be able to walk away from Sam. Not if she ever gave him that much of herself. She rode out the wave of his passion, holding him as close as she dared.

Why him? Why now? As she buried her face in the side of his neck, Clare repeated the questions that had never left her mind since meeting Sam. Why was he the one who could finally bring her to the edge of sanity? She'd known other men, but even when the sex was good, she'd never come close to climaxing.

So why Sam? Why now? Sam didn't want to love her; he wanted to fix her, change her. She felt like a fly caught in his web, unable to walk away and scared to death of being trapped.

Sam let deep breathing settle his emotions before he tried to speak. Anger mixed with the warm afterglow of climax, a climax he knew Clare hadn't shared. He felt anger at himself for not taking her with him, anger at Clare's need to control her sensual feelings, anger at the people who'd forgotten to reassure a young orphan that she was loved.

More than anything, Sam was angry that if he told

Clare he loved her, the words would send her packing. She wasn't ready for lust, much less love.

How could she ever learn to love him if her instinctive need for control kept her from trusting him? Sam clung to the hope that after that night, the sensual side of Clare's nature would be just as strong as the logical part of her soul. If he was ever going to break down the wall around her heart, he would have to fight fire with fire, instinct with instinct. He'd have to make Clare want him so badly, she'd lose herself in his arms.

Finally Sam rolled away and covered her with a light quilt. "I'll be right back."

The bed creaked slightly as Clare adjusted the geometric-patterned quilt nervously and looked at the stereo alarm beside the bed. The digital readout glowed angrily into the dark, chastising her for losing track of time. "I can't stay. It's after midnight."

Sam grinned and headed for the bathroom. "Yeah, I know. That's why you aren't going back to the house."

"What do you mean?"

"In case you've forgotten, the porch light goes out at midnight. You wouldn't want William to hit you with a baseball bat, would you?" Sam asked as he shut the bathroom door.

"I'll take my chances with William," Clare whispered, and slid off the bed, wrapping herself tightly in the quilt. "At least with him I'd know what hit me."

Before she could worry about the baseball bat, she had to find her underwear. With one eye on the bathroom door and one eye on the floor, Clare quickly circled the bed and retrieved the scrap of lace and silk. Somehow, the simple act of pulling on a pair of panties made her feel infintely less vulnerable. She readjusted the quilt and made a dash for the stairs, but didn't manage to get down them before the bathroom door opened. Clare froze with one foot on the first step and her heart in her throat.

"I guess baseball bats don't scare you," Sam observed dryly from across the room.

"Not really," Clare said in a small voice, still not moving from the stairs or turning around. He'd be naked, and she didn't want to be caught staring at him. God, she was such a coward, but if she turned around, she *would* stare, and she didn't know if she could hold back from Sam again. She couldn't afford to give him any excuse to tumble her back into bed. Not when it had taken every ounce of willpower she had to maintain control the last time.

"Maybe you're right. You don't need to worry about being whacked on the head," Sam said as he came up beside her and fingered the edge of the quilt at her back. "Considering recent events, if I were *you*—coming in after midnight wearing a gown and a smile—I'd be more worried about William counting the condoms in my nightstand than about the baseball bat."

Horrified at the thought, Clare swiveled to gape at Sam. "He wouldn't. He knows I had to come out here to get my cat. He wouldn't."

Shrugging, Sam slipped his fingers into the shadow between the quilt and her skin. "He might. If I were you, I'd stay here tonight."

Clare risked a brief glance downward to satisfy her curiosity. He hadn't pulled on a robe or a shirt, but she stopped halfway down his bare chest when he tugged experimentally on the quilt. Renewing her death grip on the ends of the quilt, she raised her eyes and an eyebrow.

"Whether I stay or not, William is still going to know I—know we—that tonight was—dammit, Sam! You know what I mean."

Grinning, Sam tried to help her out, "We made love, Clare, and I don't particularly care who knows. But William won't suspect a thing if you get up early and fetch the morning paper. What's he going to say if you come through the door with the newspaper in your hand and a bright, cheery good-morning smile on your face?"

Clare's jaw dropped for a second. "That's positively brilliant."

"Thank you. Come to bed." When she hesitated, Sam exhaled loudly. "Come to bed—*please*."

"That's not such a good idea." Clare moved down another step, but the quilt didn't. Sam had no intention of loosening his hold. His passive resistance made it quite clear that she was welcome to go downstairs, but she'd have to do it without the quilt. And when she looked over her shoulder, the glint in his eye made it quite plain that he'd watch her every move.

"Sleeping together is the best idea I've had in a long time," Sam said. "Come on, Clare. Let me hold you tonight. Just hold you. Does that break some secret rule you've made for yourself?"

"No." *It breaks all of them. I'm not supposed to want to sleep with you.*

"Then come to bed."

"My gown's downstairs."

"I don't want to sleep with your gown. I want to sleep with you. Skin to skin. Heat to heat. Get the picture?" Sam asked as he let go of the quilt.

"Vividly. You have quite a knack for making yourself understood," she assured him, suddenly goaded by the fact that he wasn't uncomfortable with the situation. As Sam backed away, she swallowed and studied her feet intently.

Once again he'd maneuvered her into a predicament that required she make a choice from two equally unsuitable options. On the one hand, she could risk William's disapproval and raised eyebrows if she returned to the house, even with her cat, at this late hour; on the other hand, she could risk another piece of her heart by sleeping in Sam's arms. Worst of all, she *wanted* to sleep in Sam's arms.

"Come to bed, Clare," he ordered softly as she heard the bedsprings complain as he settled himself.

When she turned, Sam held the covers slightly up in invitation. Still unwilling to jump so easily into his bed, she suggested, "I could sleep on the couch."

Sam's answer was as quick as his laughter, "I don't have a couch."

"Do you plan these things?" Clare asked in frustration as she gave up her position on the stairs and approached the bed. "How can you always be in the wrong place at the right time with all the clever answers?"

"Practice." He smiled suggestively. "I believe in practice."

Clare flushed with the heat his remark caused. Wetting her lips and adjusting the quilt again gave her a minute to think. Even if she did crawl into his bed, she had to tell him that what had happened between them couldn't happen again. He'd already told her he wasn't a one-night-stand kind of guy. He'd expect more from her, and she had to straighten him out now. "Listen, Sam—"

"Shh, Clare. Don't say anything. We'll sort everything out in the morning when we can think more clearly."

Inch by inch she lowered the quilt, unaware of how her nervousness mirrored a sensual striptease. Finally, Sam's patience snapped and he reached out to grab her wrist. In one fluid movement he threw back the covers and pulled Clare into his arms.

Slowly, she melted into the contours of his body, and as if they were both aware of the fragile truce that existed between their libidos, neither of them so much as wiggled afterward. Sam inhaled her fragrance and fell asleep thinking, *the sooner you go to sleep, the sooner you'll wake up with Clare in your arms.*

Clare fell asleep trying to ignore the comforting feel of Sam's strong heart beating beneath her cheek.

Clare fought her way out of the slumber that paralyzed her limbs and weighed down her eyelids. She smiled dreamily. For the first time in weeks, she managed to sleep without tossing and turning. The pillow beneath her head smelled of sunshine, detergent, and Sam.

Sam!

The gale-force winds of reality blew away the fog of sleep as Clare remembered where she slept and with whom she slept. As her eyes snapped open, she bolted upright in bed, turning her head first to check for Sam and then to read the clock. Sam was gone. *Seven-thirty!* And Sam was already up!

Oh, no, what if William was too?

"Sam!" she yelled at the closed bathroom door as she jumped out of bed and grabbed the familiar quilt. "Why didn't you wake me! God, I'm late. What time does William get up?"

She didn't wait for him to answer any of her questions. Instead, she flew down the stairs, running her fingers through her short hair to tame it. She paused in Sam's downstairs study only long enough to toss her gown over her head and grab the flamingo robe. She scooped up Slick on her way out the door.

Shifting Slick like a five-pound sack of flour, Clare maneuvered her arms into the robe and began to sprint down the driveway. A grin spread across her face, and she breathed a sigh of relief as she spotted the fat Sunday edition of the *Memphis Commercial Appeal* lying pristinely near the curb. Now she could face William. Now she had a reason for wandering around in her gown and robe.

When she had the plastic-wrapped newspaper in her hands, she slowed her pace and let herself enjoy the late spring morning. Birds twittered, and green leaves rustled with the gentle breeze. Sunshine slipped through the tree branches and dappled the lawn.

"See, Slick, everything worked out perfectly. And you were worried," Clare chided softly.

You were worried, she reminded herself. And still are. Sleeping with Sam had changed everything for her. Since her parents' death, she'd always wanted to belong in someone's life, to matter to someone. After sleeping with Sam, the need was worse, more specific. She wanted to belong in Sam's life, but he'd already admitted that he wasn't good with relationships and women. He'd let one woman walk out of his life because he didn't want her enough to change his workaholic habits.

A humorless laugh escaped Clare as she thought of the irony. She'd never fit into Sam's life because of the very workaholic habits that had broken up his previous relationship. Only this time the habits belonged to her, and Sam had already warned her that he wouldn't compromise. For him, life was too short to settle for less than what he wanted. He wasn't interested in taking a lemon and making lemonade. He wanted it all or nothing.

He hadn't actually said the words, but he was a man who wanted the total package—home, a wife who had time for fun, kids. He wasn't interested in committing to a woman who didn't or couldn't fit into his plans. He wasn't interested in a woman who was scared to make promises.

He wanted magic and surprises. Well, she didn't believe in magic, and she hated surprises. She wouldn't give up the security in her life just because a man made her toes tingle and her head spin. He was sexy, but she wasn't sure any man was worth risking her entire life. Even if he could make the lonely go away for a while.

Sleeping with Sam had definitely changed everything, and not necessarily for the better. If she were smart, she'd pack her bags quickly and run like a fox to ground. Sadly, Clare realized she wasn't smart, because she had no intention of leaving Sam's house. At least not until after Ellie's visit. If she accomplished nothing else, she intended to meet Ellie on equal footing for once, and Sam's house would do that for her. Sam's house would banish *poor Clare* from Ellie's vocabulary.

With that thought on her mind, Clare stepped into the kitchen wearing a bright, cheery smile that faded as she took in the scene before her. Sam, not William, stood in front of the stove, folding an omelet like a pro. A dish towel was draped over his shoulder, and the table was set for two.

Looking around her, Clare realized Sam had to have been up a very long time. Breakfast was almost finished, and he'd showered. After last night, she had no trouble imagining Sam in the shower with water cascading onto his back, spilling over his shoulders, and running in rivulets down his belly. Heat surged through Clare as she mentally shook her head to erase the erotic picture.

"You're up early this morning," he said without turning around. "I guess the early bird fetches the paper."

"That's worm," corrected Clare as she dropped the cat to the floor. Neon-green shorts and a muscle T-shirt made Sam's body look great. Too great, Clare decided. Too obvious. A blatant invitation for women to stare. *Now, why did it matter if women stared at Sam? Women who stared at Sam were none of her business.*

She tried to keep her voice casual as she asked, "Where's William?"

"At Rebecca's," Sam answered, and caught two pieces of toast as they shot out of the toaster. He finally turned and smiled at her, either oblivious of or ignoring the undercurrent of morning-after nervousness. "Here, butter these while they're hot."

Clare set the paper on the counter and took the toast. Suspicion lurked in her mind, nudging her to ask, "Exactly when did William decide to pay his daughter a visit?"

"About ten years ago. He likes to have Sunday breakfast with his daughter before going to church with the family." Sam slid an omelet onto her plate and pulled out her chair before putting the pan back on the stove. "Dig in. The hash browns might be a little cold."

Actually, Sam decided the hash browns were positively warm when compared to the frosty glare coming from Clare's side of the table. Trying to thaw her attitude, Sam held firmly on to his smile and tried again. "Would you care for some grits?"

"No, thank you. I've never acquired a taste for that particular southern breakfast food. White, grainy, tasteless mush isn't much of a taste treat." *Well, that was certainly rude*, Clare thought as she reached for the orange marmalade. When in doubt, nervous, or embarrassed, she tended to attack. Just then she was suffering from all three of those emotions.

Sam set the bowl of grits down and snapped his napkin across his lap. "Get up on the wrong side of the bed this morning?"

"Even worse. I got up *in* the wrong bed this morning." With more force than necessary, she unscrewed the marmalade lid and then reached for her spoon.

"Ah, I thought we'd be getting around to that soon enough. Although, I was sort of hoping we'd make it through breakfast first." The color of his eyes deepened from the warm brown of tobacco to dark shades of burnt umber and wet leather. "But since you're so eager to get it over with, and judging from last night, that's a habit of yours. Let's talk about—" Holding up his hands, Sam made little quotation marks with his index and middle fingers. "Last night."

"Let's not," Clare said quickly, embarrassment taking control of her emotions. The one thing she particularly didn't want to talk about was last night. The kitchen was suddenly warm and stuffy. Just knowing that Sam had probably analyzed every gesture, every kiss, every word was enough to make her perspire nervously. She rubbed the back of her wrist across her forehead and then dumped another spoonful of marmalade on her toast.

With forced calm, she tried to end the conversation. "What's there to say? We were curious. We're two adults. Sooner or later it was bound to happen. A simple release of tension." She scooped out a third spoon of the sweet orange spread and said, "As far as sex goes, it wasn't bad, but now we can put it behind us. Forget about it."

"Not likely," Sam said in a half-amused tone. "Are you nervous about something, or do you always have a little toast with your jelly?"

Looking down, Clare grimaced at the mountain of marmalade piled on her piece of toast.

"What are you afraid of, Clare?"

His question made her unreasonably angry. "Stop it, Sam. You're not my shrink, and I'm not afraid of anything. I happen to like orange marmalade. Anything wrong with that?"

"Oh, no. Not a thing. My mistake. I just thought you might be a little upset that last night your precious control slipped long enough for you to fall into bed with me."

Incensed, Clare dropped her spoon. "What a rotten thing to say! I did not *fall* into bed with you like some bimbo."

"Then what did you do?" When she hesitated to answer, Sam goaded, "Careful, Clare. You don't want to admit we made love. That'd be too much like admitting I get to you. And God forbid that you admit to wanting anyone. That would break McGuire's Rule."

"And what rule is that?"

"Two's a crowd."

As usual, Sam was dead on the mark. The truth of his words slammed into Clare like an unexpected punch below the belt. He enjoyed turning over the emotional rocks in her soul and exposing the hidden secrets to the harsh light of reality. She worried her bottom lip with her teeth as a gulf of silence widened between Sam's side of the table and hers. He managed to convey enormous disapproval as his words sank slowly into her heart. *Two's a crowd.*

Sam finally filled the silent void. "In case you're wondering, that pithy little rule of yours makes a lousy credo for living and a pathetic, short epitaph for a tombstone."

"How clever," Clare said as her chin came up. "You've managed to insult me in the here and the hereafter."

"I'd like to insult you forevermore, but you don't believe in tomorrow, much less happily ever after."

"I don't have much reason to believe in happily ever after."

"Fine," Sam said, and drilled her with a look so intense, Clare wanted to look away. "I won't argue that with you, I won't even ask you why you won't believe, but why the hell can't you believe in the happily right now?"

"You can't have one without believing in the other. What sane person could possibly be happy *now*, knowing they were going to be unhappy *later*?"

"How can you possibly know you're going to be unhappy later?" Sam's question was almost a shout.

"I'm always unhappy later."

"Except when you're in control."

"Except when I'm in control," she agreed, pleased

that he finally understood the benefits of organizing her life.

"So the secret to happily right now is to give you control?"

"What do you mean?" Clare asked uncertainly. Sam had that look again, and when Sam had that look, trouble was sneaking up behind her on silent feet.

"I mean," Sam clarified, "that you'd be happier about what's happening between us if you were in control."

"Nothing's happening between us, and I didn't say that."

"Yes, you did."

"No, I said—Sam, I'm not going to let you tangle me up with all this convoluted logic of yours. The bottom line is that I need your house. Period. Anything more is a bad idea. I'm not changing, and you're not changing."

"There's nothing convoluted about my logic. You said you'd be happier if you were in control. So I'm putting you in charge of this relationship. You're in control. You're in the driver's seat."

"Excuse me?" Clare asked faintly.

"You're in control. This relationship is on autopilot until you say we make love again."

"Just like that?"

"Just like that."

"You can walk away from last night?" Clare asked, suddenly unhappy with the idea.

"Let's just say that I have faith in Mother Nature."

"You shouldn't. She's a woman. She's on my side," Clare pointed out.

"I like women. I'll take my chances." Sam speared a bite of egg with his fork and settled back, quite pleased with his brilliance. Clare might not know it, but trusting

Mother Nature was the beginning of the end for her. Mother Nature never played fair. Survival of the species depended upon a woman's biological imperative to find a mate. And when Clare's biological imperative became unbearable, he fully intended to be handy.

NINE

Clare peered cautiously over the second-floor railing and scanned the entrance hall. Living in Sam's house for the past week had taught her the value of reconnaissance. The man was everywhere. And where he wasn't, his trusty scout William was. Once she confirmed that Sam wasn't lurking in the foyer, she slipped quietly down the stairs, glad she'd remembered to take off her shoes. Bare feet didn't squeak on the hardwood floors the way rubber-soled tennis shoes did.

Finding a moment's peace to work on her Japanese presentation had become a personal quest. If William wasn't feeding her, Sam was sneaking up on her, touching her, talking to her, playing practical jokes on her—like putting the local newspaper's front page over the middle pages of a Dayton, Ohio, paper. So she felt justified in not only looking around the living room before she sat down in the window seat, but looking over the edge of the sill just to be sure Sam wasn't skulking in the bushes.

Finally, Clare felt comfortable enough to settle back,

cross her legs yoga-style, and concentrate on next week's presentation. She'd put off the inevitable consultation with Sam as long as possible. Somehow, opening up her professional life to Sam's inspection was as difficult as allowing Sam into her personal life had been.

She was conscious of wanting his approval. That first night, when she confessed her secretaries didn't like her, his approving smile had filled her with warmth, making her crave more of them. He had a way of bringing the sun into a room with him. He also had a way of bringing sex into the room.

Over the past week he'd caressed her with his eyes and stripped her with his gaze. If he managed to press against her, he lingered long enough for her to feel the hardening of his body. Every look, every touch, shouted his desire, but he waited, never pushing, never asking, never demanding. He just waited and watched her.

He watched her at dinner. He watched her climb the staircase every night. He watched her get into her car every morning as he lounged against the carriage-house door and saluted her with his coffee cup. He watched her so much, she was ready to scream from the tension he created. Without a single word he repeatedly managed to tell her exactly what he wanted. He wanted to be inside her, stroking her, filling her. And all too often lately, she wanted the same thing.

Sex and Sam were becoming obsessions of hers. No doubt, that was the reason for waging his ridiculous "Look, touch, but don't consummate!" campaign. She was winning the battles, but Sam was winning the war. Clare sighed and closed her eyes against the frustration she feared had become a permanent part of her, so much so that it invaded her dreams. Last night she'd dreamed of standing in front of the bedroom window, wrapped in a plush bath towel still warm from the dryer. She could almost feel the nubby texture of the terry cloth against her damp body as she remembered the dream.

Anticipation settled heavily in her belly, urging her closer to the window. A thick satin cord pulled back the heavy drapes, and a sheer white panel floated in front of the window, shielding her, keeping her safe from prying eyes. Knowing Sam would be watching, she reached out to push back the panel that blurred her silhouette and offered her a small measure of privacy. The symbolism of sweeping away the last filmy barrier between them did not escape Clare, and her breath came in shaky half-gulps.

Even in the dark she could see Sam as he stood at the window of the carriage-house bedroom. He had one forearm propped against the frame, and he leaned his body toward the glass, never taking his eyes off her. Sam always watched, especially in the night.

Dreams weren't bound by reality, and in her fantasy she could see his eyes as they glittered hungrily. Wordlessly, he urged her to finish what she'd started when she pulled back the curtain. He smiled. Throw in the towel, Clare, he seemed to say. Give up. You know you want to.

A cool drop of water from her wet hair had trickled down her neck as she tried to decide whether or not to lower the towel. Whether or not to take the risk. She reached out, touching the pads of her fingers to the glass, absorbing the soothing feel of the windowpane. Without a word she let the towel slip to the floor. And then Sam had smiled that warm smile that filled her and made her want more.

Abruptly, her thoughts were shattered as Sam's voice

invaded her fantasy. "This is my favorite place to day-dream too."

Startled and feeling very flushed, Clare clumsily gathered up the worksheets that had slipped from her fingers to her lap. "I wasn't daydreaming!"

"Sure you were. Everybody daydreams. Fantasy is right up there with anticipation and foreplay," he told her as he slid to the floor and rested his head against the cushioned window seat. "And daydreams always show on your face, no matter how careful you think you are."

"I wasn't daydreaming," Clare insisted to his perfect profile, noticing for the first time that he had incredibly long lashes, eyelashes even Ellie would kill for.

"From your expression, you looked halfway to heaven." A smile that was more properly classified as a smirk appeared on Sam's face. "But you weren't day-dreaming. Right."

Clare grit her teeth and refused the bait. She had finally accepted the futility of arguing with him. Especially when he was right. "Did you want something in particular, or are you just here to annoy me in general?"

"William sent me to distract you. It's Friday night. He's concerned. He says you're *working* again," Sam explained in a tone that implied working at home was evil. He twisted his head so he could see Clare's reaction.

"Does the man have hidden video cameras, or what?" asked Clare in exasperation.

"Radar," Sam said sagely. "Of course, I don't have any hard evidence. I'm just relying on years of experience."

"How much I work isn't William's concern."

"Right," Sam said with a wink and a nod.

"Stop that. This is serious. Half the time the man treats me like I'm sixteen. You didn't warn me about this when I rented the house. He doesn't even ask permission to meddle in my business anymore!" Clare lowered her voice. "I shouldn't have to remind you that he put *condoms* in the nightstand, for God's sake!"

"Welcome to the family," Sam said with a chuckle as he resettled his head against the window seat.

Clare caught her breath and stared hard at Sam, who obviously saw nothing wrong with the domestic routine in the Tucker household. In fact, Sam was as bad as William. Neither of them asked permission to meddle in her business; they just did. William thought nothing of commenting on the disappointing lack of male phone callers and always within earshot of Sam. Yesterday's breakfast conversation with William had covered the length of her skirts, the clothes on the floor of her room, and the color of her nail polish, which was "too" red.

If she worked late, she was expected to call, and if she didn't work late, she was expected to come home for dinner. When she came home for dinner, she was expected to eat. William and Sam didn't seem to notice the extra five pounds, but the scales did. However, since neither Sam nor William cared about the pounds, Clare couldn't manage to care either. Sam and William had seen her at her worst, and yet her worst didn't seem to bother them.

And their concern didn't irritate her nearly as much as she liked to pretend. Lately, Clare had begun to wonder if she could go back to the quiet of her condo. *Not quiet. Emptiness.* She shook her head and told herself to snap out of it. She had no business going all sappy and soft about Sam and his life. If she didn't get a grip, pretty soon she'd start bursting into his house yelling, "Honey, I'm home."

She needed perspective. She needed Ellie to hurry up. When she'd decided to trick Ellie by appropriating Sam's house, she never imagined that the family circle would open up and pull her inside. Lately, she'd begun to wish she was more than just a challenge to Sam. Then maybe she could start believing in the magic of happily ever after.

"You're daydreaming again," Sam announced. "And don't deny it. You've daydreamed since the first moment I met you."

This time Clare didn't bother to deny his accusation. "It's not a crime."

"No, it's not," agreed Sam as he heaved himself up from the floor and joined her on the window seat. He swiveled, squared his back up against the wall opposite her, and slipped his legs on either side of hers. "What do you daydream about, Clare?"

All she could think about was that damned striptease in front of the window as she dropped the towel. She could still feel the heat from dream-Sam's eyes as he fed hungrily on the sight. She tried to swallow past the lump in her throat.

"Nothing you'd be interested in," she managed to answer by scraping together every bit of breath she had left. Sam's casual disregard of her personal space always made the bottom drop out of her stomach. He acted as if he didn't know where he left off and she began, while she knew *precisely* where his body touched hers, where the electricity began to flow, where the pulse began inside the pit of her stomach.

Sam leaned forward slightly and ran his finger down her nose and over her lips as he talked. "Keep your secrets if you want, Clare. I won't push you if you're not ready. But can't you just imagine what it would be like to share fantasies?"

His question made her heart pump in fits and starts, made her blood run hot and cold, and created an unsteadiness in her hands that made gripping the thick folder impossible.

Sam rescued the papers before they slid from her fingers. "Well, would you look at this! You have actually brought home the ultrasecret Mitsuo proposal. I was wondering when you were going to break down and let me see this . . . *encyclopedia* of facts. Lord, Clare, are all your files so thick?"

Immediately, Clare reached for the file. "I didn't bring it home for you to see."

Sam ignored her and devoured the file. "Then I'm lucky to have caught you."

"The presentation's not ready."

"They never are."

Clare gave up. Sooner or later Sam had to look at the project. Dave was paying for his help. "It's not much really. Just my cost worksheets and a rough draft of the letter of credit terms."

"And a suggested opening order, pie charts, one helluva bar graph on product performance, shipping schedules, and articles focusing on boomerang products."

"Those are components that American companies export and then buy back as a part of a finished product."

Sam briefly raised his eyes from the file. "Yeah, I know. You've been busy. You've also got a list of other Mitsuo suppliers, a list of Mitsuo Automotive subsidiaries, a culture brief on the Far East, and the tear sheets from a two-year-old trade journal, an article about Mitsuo's sports sedan and its fuel system troubles. I'll bet you got A's on your college research papers."

"Alert the media," Clare said with sarcasm. "So I like to prepare. That isn't a crime either."

Sam shook his head. "Not unless you do it after five o'clock. According to Dave, you're supposed to be learning from his mistakes. But I will admit that you've got a good start here."

"Start?" Clare wasn't sure she heard him correctly. Her file might be rough, certainly not in presentation form, but it was pretty damn complete.

"A start." Sam closed the file and handed it back. "This is just your security blanket, something to remind you of what's at stake. I guarantee that Mitsuo already knows more about Racing Specialties than you'll ever find out about them, and they aren't going to be interested in your pretty numbers and graphs this time around."

Trying not to bristle at Sam's quick dismissal of her facts and figures, Clare said, "They wouldn't come halfway around the world to shoot the breeze."

"That's exactly what they would do."

Clare digested that for a moment and said, "This is a test."

Sam touched his nose and pointed at her. "Bingo. You got it in one."

"Dave was so sure they were ready to do some business."

"They're ready to do some business, all right. They're just not sure with whom. Price is important, but so is the business relationship."

"Okay, expert, what do I do if I'm not going to dazzle them with charts and graphs?"

"First, you don't push—"

"Funny advice coming from you," Clare couldn't resist commenting.

Sam continued as if she hadn't said a word. "Let them ease into the relationship. Have business cards printed in both languages."

"Japanese *and* English?"

"One language on each side. You get brownie points for extra effort. Get the university to help you with the translation." Sam paused, bit his lip in thought, and then continued. "Okay, next—Mitsuo's president and I have mutual friends. To be on the safe side of the etiquette fence, I should be the one to pick them up at the airport and bring them to you."

Clare laughed. "You wouldn't by any chance be giving me the seal of approval with your little chauffeur act?"

"That's exactly what I'll be doing. An introduction through an intermediary is going to be a lot more helpful to you than a cold handshake and a bilingual card. It's the international version of the good-ol'-boy network."

"Now, why don't I have any trouble believing you are an expert in the good-ol'-boy school of business?"

Slowly, Sam leaned forward, framing her drawn-up knees with his, and resting his forearms on their knees. "Do you want to hear this or not?"

Clare swallowed again as she realized exactly how much of Sam's body was in contact with hers. Somehow her toes had worked their way beneath an extremely warm and sensitive part of his anatomy. Before she could answer, Sam scooted back, untangled his legs, and stood up suddenly.

"I can't believe I'm even discussing this. It's Friday night, and I refuse to discuss business strategy on date night, woman. Get some shoes and let's go."

"Go? Go where?" Clare swiveled and let her feet drop to the floor.

Pleased, Sam noted that she hadn't made the usual excuses. For the first time she was more interested in *where* they were going than in *why* she couldn't go. "I promised my nephews I'd take them to a movie. You can help me protect the other people in the theater from the little savages."

Clare took his offered hand and let him pull her up. "How savage can they be? I saw the pictures in your room. They're both in school. They should be somewhat trained by now."

"They should be, but Pamela is a lousy disciplinarian. She believes in letting children express their innermost self. I, on the other hand, would prefer it if they didn't express themselves with popcorn fights."

Hugging her file to her chest, Clare wondered how much of what Sam said was the truth. In their school pictures the boys looked like angels. Shiny blond hair, brown eyes, and wide smiles full of teeth. No, she didn't quite see them as monsters. Unless they got bored with the movie. Cautiously, she asked, "What movie?"

"Bimbo Ninjas."

A giggle escaped her before she managed to school her expression into one of disappointment. "Oh. I was hoping we could see that new vampire flick—*Hunks That Go Bump in the Night.*"

Sam didn't bother to hold back the laughter. He

pulled her into his arms, file and all. *"Hunks That Go Bump in the Night?"*

She shrugged. She didn't want to say anything. Not now. Not just yet. She wanted to let Sam's magic warm her. She wanted to belong to Sam and the moment for a while longer.

As his laughter faded to a chuckle, Sam felt complete for the first time in a long time. Affection, love, and laughter were back in the house again. He could enjoy some of the memories he had put away as too painful. Memories of his mother and father holding each other, his dad rocking his mother gently back and forth. For too long those memories had mocked the choices he'd made in life, and now those memories encouraged him, promised him that organized, precise Clare McGuire was worth the effort.

Chuckles gave way to quiet sighs of good humor, and Sam's good humor gave way to the desire he'd denied for the past week. Any doubts he had about disguising his need to kiss her were gone the moment she raised her chin a fraction of an inch. In silent invitation she dropped her gaze to his mouth and then slowly brought her eyes back to his. Sam wished she were issuing the silent invitation on purpose; he would have accepted with pleasure. But he knew better than to believe everything he saw.

Before he broke his promise about giving her control in the relationship, Sam stepped away, wishing he hadn't noticed the fragrance of spiced apples underscoring the perfume she wore. He had a hard enough time keeping his hands off her without remembering the way her body played peek-a-boo with a bubble bath. Deliberately, he dropped his arms. "We've got to hurry if we're going to pick up the kids and catch an early show."

Clare tried not to frown as he stepped away. She'd been almost sure he was finally going to break down and kiss her. In fact, she'd been counting on it. Some newly discovered part of her heart wanted Sam to give up before she did. Her body had turned traitor because Mother Nature slipped a joker in the deck. His name was Sam.

Dropping her file onto the window seat, Clare made a decision. "Let's go."

"Not yet." Sam pointed downward. "Shoes, Clare. You know—the leather things that go on your feet?"

"Oh, shoes! I forgot." Clare hurried toward the entrance hall. "I'll only be a minute."

"Good," Sam said as she left the room. Then added, "Any longer than that, and I'm coming after you."

As Sam raised his hand to knock on Pamela's door, Clare's heart beat more rapidly than she wanted to admit. Meeting Sam's sister wasn't a big deal, she told herself. Pamela would probably love any woman who agreed to take her kids to the movies. Hadn't her own aunt always jumped at every chance to unload her daughter and niece for an evening? What mother wouldn't want a few hours of peace and quiet?

"Cheer up," Sam whispered in her ear. "She won't bite."

Clare dredged up a smile. "No, but after listening to you, I suspect her kids do."

"Do what?" the grinning woman asked as she opened the door. She looked like a petite, pretty version of Sam.

Except her tawny mane was tamed and pulled back into a beribboned ponytail.

"Bite," Sam answered with a straight face, and ignored the flustered gasp from the woman at his side. "Clare thinks your kids might bite her."

Without blinking or missing a beat, Pamela turned to Clare. "And you came anyway! What a good sport. Sam's other girlfriends were never any fun. Of course, the boys were younger and not nearly as well-trained then. A lot younger. It has been such a long time since anyone would go out with Sam. I was afraid he'd forgotten how to . . ." Pamela winked. "Well, you know."

Now it was Sam's turn to choke and Clare's chance to twist the knife. She nodded sadly. "Oh, so *that* explains the problem."

Pamela's grin broadened and she said, "I like this one, Sam."

"Of course you do. You think you've found a partner in crime," Sam told her as he pushed Clare through the door.

"I think you've found a partner," Pamela quietly corrected him, looking from one to the other as they passed her. As she shut the door and followed them into the den, she said, "My God, look at the two of you. If William were beside you, you'd be a movie poster for *The Good, the Bad, and the Ugly!*"

Clare stopped right in the middle of sitting down and stared uncomfortably at Sam, noticing his clothes for the first time. The thin, braided leather belt through the loops of his jeans added the only bit of color to his clothes—jeans so faded they could be called white, an immaculate white rugby shirt with the sleeves pushed up, and his favorite white leather tennis shoes. Unintentionally, Clare had chosen black—black jeans, black loafers, black shirt, black onyx earrings, even the postage-stamp-sized purse she had with her was black.

"Well, I guess we know who's 'the good' and who's 'the bad,' " Sam said with a grin as he fell back into the overstuffed pillows of the couch. "I'm not sure William is going to appreciate being cast as 'the ugly' though."

"Then don't tell him," Pamela advised loudly over the sound of cowboys and Indians coming down the hall.

"Uncle Sam! Uncle Sam!" Two small blond bodies screamed as they sprinted into the room and leapt into his lap. At the words, Clare's mouth fell open and she looked at Pamela. Somehow she'd never connected the fact that Sam had nephews with the fact that they would call him *Uncle Sam*.

"Isn't it a hoot?" Pamela grinned happily. "One of the main reasons I had children was to hear those two words. You know, since the boys were born, I have never seen Sammy wear red, white, and blue."

Sam glared at her over the boys' heads while trying to answer the questions that were being thrown at him. When they settled enough to notice a stranger in the room, Sam made the introductions and was surprised to find that Clare charmed the boots and moccasins off the boys by being properly frightened of the green garden snake that was shoved in her face. Winking at Pamela, she told them their snake was about the scariest example of a garden snake she'd ever seen, and Sam realized his nephews were completely under her spell.

"Oops," Pamela said. "I should have warned you. They found him this morning. And he goes back right now," she said sternly to the boys. "We agreed."

"Ah, Mom, do we have to?" asked the younger one.

"That's where we were going when we saw Uncle Sam's car," the older one explained very primly, as though he were disappointed that his mother hadn't realized this fact.

"Come on, men," Sam said, pushing up off the sofa. "I'll go with you, and you can show me the new tree house."

"Yeah, we'll show you the tree house *and* the new tent" was echoed excitedly by both boys as they rushed out of the room with Sam in tow. They took the chaos with them, leaving quiet behind with Clare and Pamela.

"Sam didn't tell me you liked children," Pamela said, and appropriated Sam's vacated spot on the sofa.

"What's not to like?" Clare asked.

"Let's see," Pamela teased as she made a pretense of patting her pockets as though she were looking for something. "Where did I put that list?"

"Careful. You'll have me believing everything Sam says about the boys if you keep that up."

"Believe him. They're little heathens. We're hoping for a girl this time."

Startled, Clare shifted her gaze to her hostess's trim waistline. "You're pregnant?"

"Six weeks."

"Sam never said a word."

"That's because he doesn't know. We haven't told him or the boys yet."

Clare smiled; she didn't know what else to do. She'd never been the recipient of family confidences before, and she wasn't quite sure what was expected of her. Each day sank her a little deeper into the fabric of Sam's life. Everyone around him seemed to accept that she belonged. Everyone but Clare herself.

"I'm the world's worst hostess," Pamela said suddenly. "Here I am boring you to death with my news, and I haven't even offered you something to drink or eat."

"You're not boring me, and to be perfectly truthful, I couldn't eat a bite if you paid me."

"Has William been force-feeding you?" asked Pamela.

"Every chance he gets," groaned Clare. "Living in Sam's house is hard on the nerves and worse on the waistline."

Pamela smiled and pulled an imaginary piece of lint from the sofa back. "You know I'm very happy about you and Sam."

Stunned, Clare looked away briefly and then back at warm, tobacco-brown eyes that were obviously a Tucker family characteristic. The resemblance between the siblings was more than physical, Pamela had that shoot-from-the-hip attitude. She even had the same tendency to jump to the wrong conclusions. Clare met her gaze squarely and said, "I don't know what Sam's told you—"

"Not nearly enough," Pamela assured her. "But I'm not deaf or blind. I've wanted to thank you for a while now."

"For what?" Shifting uncomfortably, Clare shook her head. "I haven't done anything."

Pamela leaned over and briefly squeezed Clare's wrist. "Oh, but you have. You've given me Sam back. When Pop died, so did a part of Sam. Of course, he'd never admit it. He's much too strong for that. But inside he was missing a little spark he used to have. And now he has that again. Thanks to you."

A frown drew Clare's eyebrows together. "I didn't—"

An unladylike snort cut her off. "You did. Good God, Clare, can't you see the difference in him? When Pop killed himself, all Sammy could think about was how he'd failed, about how he'd made all the wrong choices with his life. It's very difficult for a man who's made a great deal of money to admit that he's been a failure at life."

Clare held herself very still, as if by moving she might scare away the answers she'd been looking for. "I didn't do anything. He'd already changed his life before he met me."

"Even when he turned his life around, he was still only going through the motions. He wanted a generic two point five kids, a comfortable wife, and a dog." Pamela grinned a cat-lapping-cream grin. "Now he wants you. And there's not a thing generic about you, my dear. You're so wrong for him that you're perfect."

Before Clare could frame an answer, chaos erupted in the household again as Tim, the younger boy, skidded into the room. "Mama! Aunt Clare! Come quick! The tent sort of fell down, and Uncle Sam's inside it."

Sam checked his watch as he unlocked the front door. "Eleven fifty-five."

"Let's just hope your watch isn't slow." Hiding a grin, Clare followed him inside. One of the high points of her evening had been watching Sam struggle out of the heavy canvas tent while trying to explain how it had fallen. "The last thing you need after tonight is William's wrath or anything else coming down on your head."

He shot her an unappreciative look as he crossed the threshold. "That's about enough out of you."

"Don't be so touchy," she advised. "Can I help it if my aunt liked to send me to camp to get rid of me? So, I'm a better Boy Scout than you are. The world has not stopped revolving."

"I didn't *need* your help. I would have gotten the tent up eventually."

Clare tossed her purse on the entryway table and mumbled, "Maybe when the boys were old and gray."

Turning back from his purposeful march toward the kitchen, Sam asked, "What?"

"I said—maybe we can take the boys to a movie another day."

Sam didn't look completely convinced, but after what looked like a momentous struggle with himself, he simply said, "Good night, Clare."

"Good night, Sam," she called softly, and bounded up the steps two at a time.

As she showered, Clare wondered how a simple outing to the movies could have gone so far astray of the original plan. While they'd fussed with the tent, the night had slipped away from them, and it had been after eleven o'clock before the boys remembered the movie. If Clare regretted anything about the evening, it was that she wouldn't be around to give the boys a rain check on the movie. Being with Pamela and her kids had been so easy, so natural.

Sighing and telling herself not to romanticize family life, Clare reached for the faded black shirt hanging on the back of the bathroom door. No matter how often she put Sam's shirt in the hamper, it reappeared on the peg, freshly laundered. What Clare couldn't figure out was exactly who kept putting the shirt back—William or Sam?

Last night she'd given up and slept in it. The soft cotton hugged her body and made her feel less lonely. Wearing the shirt was her reward to herself for resisting Sam and temptation. Kind of like having a bowl of ice cream as a reward for refusing cake.

Clare fastened the last button and reached for her purse to get her mother's wedding ring, which she'd taken off when she and the boys decided to dig a rain run-off trench around the tent. "Damn," she muttered. The purse was downstairs on the table.

If she left it there, she'd get an earful from William when she went down for breakfast the next morning. He'd hold up the purse by its thin strap, look at her, and inform her that he had a great many more important things to do than pick up after her all day. Groaning, she left her room and hurried down the stairs.

As she scooped the purse up from the hall table, she heard a thump from the kitchen and Slick's soft meow. "Double damn," she whispered. William liked the cat, but he absolutely drew the line at animals on the kitchen counter. Sighing, she decided she'd better go and check for footprints.

Quickly, she padded toward the kitchen, slowing when she saw the glow that illuminated the darkness. Reaching the doorway, she found Sam, still dressed in jeans and rugby shirt, holding open the refrigerator door, and bent double—his head stuck inside. Slick wove a lazy figure eight around Sam's ankles. Obviously the two were partners in this midnight raid on the kitchen. Discreetly, she cleared her throat. "Ahem."

Sam's body jerked backward. He straightened like a cat burglar with his hand caught in a jewelry case, and whirled around. Relief flooded his face when he saw her. "Don't scare me like that. I thought you were William."

"Stealing anything good?" she asked playfully as she crossed the cool linoleum to peer into the refrigerator. She found she had to maneuver around him.

Sam let her wander between the open refrigerator and his body as she inspected the contents. He noted her silk gown had been replaced by his shirt, and at the moment he was irrationally jealous of his own shirt. When he had her right where he wanted her, he leaned one hand casually on the door and the other on the side, neatly boxing her in as she turned to face him. "The only thing I have any intention of stealing at the moment is a kiss."

Suiting action to words, Sam closed the distance between them and dragged his bottom lip against the bow of her mouth. At the first touch of his lips to hers, the hunger that had driven him back to the kitchen changed. He suddenly wanted more than food for the body; he wanted food for the soul. He pulled at her lips again and willed her to respond.

Clare's eyelids dipped beneath an unexplainable weight that pushed them relentlessly toward her cheeks. Without a word Sam asked her to surrender, to throw in the towel, just like in her dreams. When he pulled back, taking his mouth from hers, Clare kept her eyes closed and ran her tongue across her top lip, tasting his kiss again, tasting her own surrender.

She no longer cared about winning the war between

them. All she could think about was losing the battle. Cold air teased her bare legs but couldn't cool the fire ignited by Sam's gentle kiss. She burned like an ember given a breath of oxygen, and the flames licked greedily at her self-control, begging for more.

TEN

When Clare opened her eyes, Sam saw the tug-of-war going on inside her. She was struggling with the feelings of contentment and passion, afraid she'd have to sacrifice one for the other. He'd always known she was intelligent, independent, and sexy. But tonight he'd seen the other qualities she kept hidden beneath her protective armor: a caring nature and a love of children.

"I made a promise, and I don't go back on my promises lightly," he told her softly as he hooked two fingers in the unbuttoned V of the black shirt she wore. Slowly, he pulled her away from the open refrigerator. When he shut the door, he added, "You're going to have to ask me this time."

Softly, in a whisper, Clare asked, "How can I ask you for anything when I don't even know what I want?"

"Ah, Clare," he chastised her gently, aching to squeeze her against his chest so tightly that she'd become a part of him. "You know what you want. Give yourself permission to feel passion. Ask, for God's sake! If you don't trust me, then trust yourself."

"I never trust myself when you're in the room," Clare admitted, allowing Sam to pull her along as he backed out of the kitchen and down the hall toward the staircase. "Right now all I can think about is the bed upstairs. And that you've never made love in it."

A stab of triumph shot through Sam and faded to a pulse of urgency. "And all I can think about is you in that bathtub, your skin soft and slick with bath oil. Do you have any idea how badly I wanted to smooth my hands over you? Do you? Ask me to put my hands on you, Clare."

She gasped, her eyes locked on his hands as he slid them to her wrists and pulled her up the stairs. Hands that were so big, so rough, so seductive, so gentle. The sight of his hands painted a vivid image of his fingers gliding up over her collarbones and down the center of her throat to outline her nipples before he swirled his palms over the sides of her breasts and lower. Suddenly she realized that as long as Sam used touch as a way of communication, she would be fascinated by and drawn to his hands. The idea hypnotized her almost as much as the imagery of his eyes in her fantasy, when he asked her to give in, to throw in the towel.

Gathering all her courage together, Clare paused at the top of the staircase, resisting the overpowering urge to tell Sam about her dream. Instead, she lifted one of his hands to her lips and slowly, deliberately, wrapped her mouth around his index finger. She had an idea what the sucking motion would do to Sam's composure, but she was startled to feel the tightening of her own belly at the erotic action. She never dropped her eyes from his as her tongue laved and sucked his finger.

"Close enough," Sam whispered hoarsely, and pulled

his hand back long enough to scoop her up in his arms, striding down the hall to his room. "I always preferred *show* over *tell*."

This time he didn't seduce her with anticipation, nor did she want him to tease her with promises of more. She wanted it all, and she wanted it all now. Sam had already kicked off his shoes before he laid her on the bed. His shirt and jeans followed, leaving his body naked except for a pair of his infamous boxers.

Clare smiled at the flamingo motif and began unbuttoning her shirt.

"Recent purchase," Sam said as the boxers joined the cast-off clothing on the floor. "They reminded me of you." He stripped his shirt from Clare's body and tossed it behind him. "Not that I need reminders. I remember this." Sam pulled her into his arms. "And this." He kissed her long and hard.

As he pushed her back onto the bed and joined her, Clare was already lost in sensation, lost in the need to end the tension of the last week. Sam pressed feather kisses down her body and stripped off her black lace panties. He seemed fascinated with the shape of her legs and the sensitive skin behind her knees. His fingers brushed along her legs, against her tender inner thighs as he separated them, and when his tongue touched her sensitive core, Clare thought she might come apart.

"Sam," she warned as she tried to move away from his intimate touch.

"Clare, *yes*." His words whispered against the triangle of curls, and his strong hands reached to span her waist, holding her. "Tonight we do this my way."

Unable to fight the desire to feel completion spill through her, Clare opened herself to his touch. Suddenly her body was no longer hers. Instinct had replaced rational thought, and she wanted Sam to finish what he'd started. When unfamiliar feelings began to coil tightly inside her, she drew a ragged breath and tensed. It was as if the world narrowed to Sam's touch and the promise of pleasure that hovered at the edge of her awareness.

"Sam!"

Her quietly desperate cry caused Sam's manhood to jerk in response. This was the Clare he wanted, reaching for him, warm with passion and uncontrolled, but he reluctantly pulled away before he pushed her over the edge. He wanted Clare to fall off the world, but he wanted to be inside her when she did.

Shifting his position, Sam sat up, reached for the bedside table, and allowed himself a small smile for William's foresight. When Clare took the foil packet out of his hand, Sam closed his eyes, afraid that the sight of her hands on him might undo what little command he had over his passion.

As she tore open the foil, Clare's body hummed with the promises made by Sam's mouth and hands. Her fingers tingled from the contact with his hard shaft as it pulsed in her hand. When she finished, she twined her fingers in his hair and pulled his lips to hers, catching and sucking on his tongue as he explored her mouth.

When Sam shifted to separate her legs, Clare felt the roughness of his thigh against her smooth-shaven one. Once again she opened to him, welcoming him, wanting him. Clare tried not to break the kiss, but a sigh escaped her as Sam entered her. She could feel the shudder in his arm muscles as he tried to hold himself completely still. He couldn't. Nor did she want him to.

Groaning, Sam rose, still kneeling on the bed, and

lifted Clare's hips to meet his thrusts. Each time he filled her, he let his thumb brush against the sensitive nub hidden in the valley beneath her springy feminine curls.

"Look at me, Clare. I want you to watch," he commanded softly, his voice ragged as he held back his climax.

At his words, Clare's eyes flew open and she saw the hunger glittering dangerously in Sam's gaze as he raised his eyes from their joining to her face. *All the better to see you with*. In that moment, Clare gave in and fell off the edge, reaching for Sam and spinning into a vortex of pleasure and completion.

Sam joined her in passion, holding on to her as if he'd never let her go. When the world settled quietly around them, Sam knew he never would let her go. She belonged with him whether or not she could admit it. She belonged in this house, in his bed, in his life. This obsessed company controller, a woman he would have bet his last dollar would be all wrong for him, was the answer to the gaping, lonely hole in his life. She made him forget about the past and think about the future he wanted.

He kissed her lightly, not forcing her to talk, and eased himself off the bed for a quick trip to the bathroom. The clothes strewn along the way affirmed his conviction that Clare belonged in his life. His bedroom floor looked like a chess board of white and black chess pieces. The battle was waged between black lace panties and white flamingo-flecked boxer shorts. His white polo shirt guarded his tennis shoes, and Clare's black jeans protected the black bra Slick once proudly paraded through her living room.

Watching him go, Clare struggled for breath, and not just because he was gorgeous. Because he'd be back. And then he'd want to talk, and she didn't want to talk. Not about tonight, not about tomorrow. She wanted to find a safe place to hide, a place to think.

Her emotions and common sense had scattered when he awakened her body to passion. She'd had to remind herself that Sam wasn't permanent. His family wasn't hers. It never would be. Sam didn't want *her*; he wanted to play the professor to her Eliza Doolittle. He wanted a Clare he'd changed and carefully molded to fit his life. Once the thrill of meeting the challenge had worn off, he'd be looking for a polite way to fade out of her life.

To Sam, the last weeks had been a game, a Good Samaritan project. He'd taught her how to want people in her life again, and that scared the hell out of her. The funniest part was that she liked the domestic bliss she found in Sam's house. She liked the way William fussed over her, scolding her as though he really cared. And she discovered, much to her dismay, she wasn't ready to give up playing house with Sam even though she knew it would have to end.

When Sam returned to bed, he found Clare huddled beneath the covers. Without a word he slid in beside her, not offering to return to the carriage house. If he did, she'd agree in a New York minute. So, he wasn't offering. He'd spent his last night alone. If she wanted him out, she'd have to bring up the subject herself.

"Good night, sweet Clare," he said as he turned to her, curling around her spoon fashion.

Predictably, Clare stiffened. "You can't *sleep* here. What will William say?"

" *'It's about damn time.'* Go to sleep, Clare."

Slowly, she relaxed in his arms, but Sam wasn't sure if she had decided William would approve, or if she was too tired to argue. He didn't care which. Either way, he was spending the night in his bed with the woman he loved. Tomorrow would take care of itself. It always did.

Morning light filtered through the sheer curtains as Clare's eyes fluttered open. She felt someone staring at her, and as her eyes focused, she saw that it was Sam. He leaned over and kissed the tip of her nose just as if he did that every morning. Memories of the night before flooded her consciousness, setting off butterflies of doubt in her stomach. Clare ran her fingers through her hair and mumbled an uncertain "Good morning."

"Good morning." For a few seconds Sam simply absorbed the moment, savoring the fact she'd lost herself in his arms and given him the gift of intimacy. "God help me, but I love you, Clare McGuire," he said, surprising even himself with the strength of feeling revealed in his voice.

The vague uneasiness Clare had felt as she struggled out of the cloud of slumber suddenly exploded into sharp pain, and she pulled away from his embrace. The thought of Sam loving her was a cruel carrot dangling in front of her nose, when she knew he was only in love with the idea of changing her, of playing the professor in a 1990's version of *Pygmalion*. Without thinking, she said, "You're not supposed to love me."

Stunned, Sam didn't try to drag her back into his arms. *You're not supposed to love me.* "What the hell did your aunt and uncle do to you?"

"Nothing. They took care of me. Just drop it, Sam. Don't read more into last night than was really there. I don't believe in love. Not in the kind that lasts. Not for me. It never does, and I'd rather not have my heart broken again."

"I'd rather not—" echoed Sam. "*I'd rather not?* Like you have a choice about loving me?" Now Sam did drag her back into his arms, slanting his body across hers and pinning her between his chest and the mattress. He shook his head and said calmly, "Two steps forward and one step back. I hate to be the one to break the news, but you can't control love. We're talking knee-jerk reaction here. Yes or no. Black or white. You either do or you don't. If you have to think about it, you probably do. Do you love me, Clare?"

Before she could answer, the bedroom door crashed open and a breathy female voice called, "Surprise, Cousin dear! Rise and shine— Oh, my, I can see you're already up. And I can only assume that he is too."

The silence following the words was so complete, the sound of a pin dropping on a carpet would have made a deafening noise. Without looking around, Sam mouthed the word *Ellie*?

Clare nodded grimly while Sam pursed his lips in a vain attempt to prevent a grin. Narrowing her eyes in warning at Sam, Clare desperately racked her brain for something witty to say and cursed fate for having to greet her cousin while wearing nothing more than yesterday's makeup. Anyone with a shred of compassion or decency would have said, "Excuse me!" and shut the door. Not Ellie. This nightmare was her punishment for trying to impress her cousin with Sam's house.

"Clare? That *is* you beneath the gorgeous blond hunk, isn't it? The man downstairs, the one who picked me up at the airport, said I should come right up. I guess he didn't know you were . . . entertaining."

A groan escaped Clare as she remembered that nothing, *absolutely nothing*, fazed Ellie. With great care Clare shoved Sam off, pulling the sheet up under her arms in the process. Stoically, she sat up and faced the music. "Hello, Ellie. You're early. I didn't think you were going to be here until next week."

"Do tell," commented Ellie with a perfectly arched brow. "Schedule change, dearie. Forget about me. Look who's been sleeping in your bed! Let's talk about him."

Sam scooted back against the headboard and settled the sheet across his lap. The indignity of being caught with his pants down didn't bother him at all, Clare noted. She wondered what he saw when he looked at Ellie. To fill the silence, she began an introduction, "He's—"

Interrupting, Sam met Ellie's inquisitive eyes with a grin and said, "I'm the boarder, Sam Tucker. I usually have to sleep in the carriage house, but Clare throws in three meals a day as part of the deal." At that moment a furry gray missile sped through the room and landed in the middle of his chest with a commanding yowl. Sam shifted the cat and said, "This is Slick. You've already met William, our butler."

"He's not *our* butler. He's yo—" Clare stopped short of blowing the entire charade, and then was sorry she'd caught her mistake in time. A part of her wanted to confess everything and get it over with.

Ellie leaned against the door facing and gave Clare a mock frown. "Cousin dear, is there something you want to tell me? You've obviously been holding out on me. Of course, you've always been a lousy pen pal. If your letters had been any more vague, they'd have been transparent."

"At least I wrote," Clare said sweetly.

"Two points," Ellie acknowledged with a grin, and

put two strokes on an imaginary scoreboard. "But I did send a Christmas card and a birthday present last year."

"Ladies," Sam said, his tone amused. "I'd love to stay and referee. But this is Saturday morning, and I'm going to be late for a class. Ellie, I wouldn't want to shock you by getting out of bed naked, so if you could give us a few minutes alone?"

"For you—Sam, was it?—I'd give just about anything." Then Ellie pointed a finger at Clare. "I'll give *you* five minutes to get downstairs and start spilling your guts. Any longer, and I'll have to assume you need rescuing from this Nordic stranger."

Ellie's bright, cheerful laughter echoed down the hall as she left them alone. For a moment Clare almost saw the humor of the situation. At least until she saw the look on Sam's face, a look that warned her to tread carefully.

"This isn't finished, Clare. Settle the past with your cousin and figure out what you want. When Ellie leaves, I want an answer."

It wasn't until Sam left that Clare realized he hadn't shown the slightest interest in tall, blond, healthy Ellie. He hadn't stared, stammered, or drooled.

"Ellie?" Rubbing her hands against her jeans, Clare looked into the empty living room. "Where are you?"

"In the kitchen," Ellie called out. "William's making iced tea." As Clare entered the room, Ellie said, "He makes ice cubes out of tea. That way the melting ice doesn't water down the tea! Oh, of course, you know that," she said with a sheepish grin. "He works for you."

"He doesn't work for me," Clare snapped, suddenly unwilling to lie in front of William. "He works for Sam.

This is Sam's house. These are Sam's antiques. Even the damned ice cubes belong to Sam. I live in a condominium with comfortable furniture that's old, but not by any stretch of the imagination antique! I borrowed all of this"—Clare waved a hand—"to impress you."

"What?" Ellie tilted her head in confusion. "Slow down! You've lost me."

"She said she was a guest in this house," William clarified forcefully. "Do you want some tea or not?"

"Yes, please," Ellie whispered as she sat down at the kitchen table. Obligingly, William banged a glass of tea down in front of her. Ellie's fingers slid around the glass in a reflexive action as she continued to stare at Clare. "None of this is yours? But your letters, and Mama said—"

"What she wanted to believe," Clare interrupted. "And what I let her believe." Turning to William, who didn't seem the least horrified by what he'd heard, Clare said, "My mouth's suddenly dry. Could I have some of that tea?"

"Only if you promise to drink it somewhere else," William grumbled. "I don't want the two of you cluttering up my kitchen all day while you figure out your life history. I got things to do besides listen to your problems." William handed her the tea and hustled her out of the kitchen along with Ellie, who sputtered disapproval.

"Lord, Clare. I can't believe you put up with that behavior from a servant. The way he acts, you'd think he owned the place. He ought to be fired."

"You can't fire family," Clare said as she entered the living room. She curled up in the corner of the sofa before adding, "But Sam and I have considered killing him. Listen, I'm sorry about this morning and the misunderstanding. William wasn't aware of—didn't know that—"

"You were sleeping with Sam?" Ellie finished helpfully as she sat down. "Good, I'd hate to think the old guy knew everything. While I waited for you, he looked at me with that judgmental expression. I was trying to figure out if I came up short in his opinion. I'm pretty sure I did."

Clare looked skeptical. "Ellie Jordan worried about making a good impression?"

"Sure, doesn't everybody?"

"Not Ellie Jordan. I didn't think you worried about anything." Clare pulled a magazine closer to the edge of the cherry coffee table and set her tea glass on it. "Least of all people's impressions of you."

Widening her eyes in disbelief, Ellie said, "What rock have you been living under? My whole life has been a struggle to make a good impression. I grew up in the house with quiet, well-mannered *Clare*, who never did anything wrong. The perfect child, invisible and undemanding."

"You were afraid of being compared to me?" Clare asked, doubt heavily coloring her words. "I don't believe you."

"Believe me." Ellie kicked off her soft leather flats and tucked her feet beneath her. Suddenly she asked, "Do you know why I wanted to come and see you?"

"Not a clue," Clare admitted warily.

For the first time, the laughter that always sparkled in Ellie's eyes dimmed, and she poked at the ice in her glass with a pink manicured nail. "I wanted to see if you were still as good at controlling your life. To see if you were happier than me."

"To see if I was happier?" Clare echoed.

"I figured you had to be." Ellie shrugged. "I always envied you. You didn't have to be the bone Mama and Daddy fought over. No one expected you to choose between them. You could do whatever you wanted and no one bothered you. Sometimes I wish they'd gone ahead with the divorce."

"They were going to get divorced?" With a few short sentences Ellie had rewritten history, making Clare doubt her naive conclusions about her place in the family. Had she mistaken their preoccupation with a disintegrating marriage for disinterest in her?

"Now it's too late for divorce," Ellie continued. "They don't like each other, but neither of them has the courage to walk away. Christmas is the worst. You're lucky. You don't have to go."

"Too late for a divorce?"

Ellie's head snapped up, and she stared at Clare. "What is wrong with you? Stop repeating everything I say in that stunned tone. None of this is exactly shocking news."

A shiver raced over Clare as she whispered, "Maybe not to you, but I didn't know any of this."

"You didn't know! Come on, Clare. Your parents loved each other. Couldn't you see the difference between mine and yours?"

"Obviously not," Clare answered, her mind racing through years of memories, re-evaluating those memories.

Ellie's expression shifted from disbelief to stunned acceptance. "Maybe you couldn't. You were only seven when you came to live with us. By the time you were old enough to know what was going on, they stopped talking about divorce, but nothing was ever really the same."

For the first time, Clare realized that growing up had been just as difficult for her cousin. Her parents hadn't died, but her life hadn't been any happier. "Poor Ellie."

"Right. Poor Ellie. Poor little rich girl. Every time I hear those words I want to scream, because it's true. I run like hell from any man who might be serious. I'm scared to death of marriage. Sometimes I wonder if I'll ever be happy. How about you? Did you escape the curse? Are you happy, Clare?" she asked softly. "Is your life under control?"

Clare turned off the Spitfire's ignition and stared up at Sam's house, sorry that Ellie's visit was over. In thirty-six hours they'd taken a second look at their childhoods and managed to forge a relationship. As crazy as it seemed, Ellie was suddenly family, someone to be missed. And now that her cousin was safely on a plane, it was time to start living in the real world again.

Sam's house wasn't hers. She had to go back to the condo, back to life before Sam and William. Resigned to that fact, Clare got out of the car and walked to the house. When she pushed open the back door, she found William rummaging in the pantry and up to his elbows in canned goods. Laughing, she announced her arrival, "Hey, I'm home."

He looked up briefly and said, "I hope you remembered to tip the porter. That woman has more luggage than a department store."

"Her name is *Ellie*." Clare tossed her purse on the

table. "What on earth are you doing in there? Alphabet-izing?"

William straightened and slowly turned to look at her. "Before you came in here to waste my time, I was figuring out what we need from the grocery."

Properly chastised but grinning, Clare reached for the pad and pencil on the table. "You tell me what you want, and I'll make a list."

When William left for the store a half hour later, Clare realized she wasn't acting like someone on the verge of leaving. In fact, she'd added Kitty Litter and cat food to the list without thinking. A part of her wanted to believe she wasn't leaving, that Sam loved *her* and not the idea of *changing* her. The other part kept waiting for the shoe to drop, for the silver lining to develop a tear. She hadn't taken a risk with her emotions in so long, she was afraid she'd forgotten how.

And until one part or the other won the tug-of-war, she was stuck on the fence, trapped by doubts. Why couldn't she believe in his love? What was holding her back? What was missing?

For a long time she sat staring at the pad in front of her, drawing doodles with the pencil and trying to make up her mind about Sam. As she thought, she divided the paper down the middle and labeled the left side with the word *for* and the right side with the word *against*. Across the top she wrote *Loving Sam*.

After an hour of soul-searching she was no closer to an answer. Clare gave up and went searching for Sam instead. She found him sprawled across her bed, taking a nap with Slick. Even sleeping he was sexy. He lay on his back, one foot tucked under the opposite knee, and one arm flung over his eyes. Slick nestled in the crook of his other arm.

Quietly, Clare wrapped her arms around the bedpost and leaned her cheek against the cool, smooth wood. She couldn't come to terms with her feelings for Sam, but neither could she deny the quickening of her pulse when she looked at the bed and remembered. Just the thought of his hand moving down her belly sent heat cascading through her.

"Ellie gone?" Sam asked huskily, and adjusted his arm to cradle his head.

"Yes. I didn't mean to wake you."

Sam grinned wickedly. "You could wake the dead. Come here. I've missed you." Sam shoved the cat off the bed and reached for her. Clare hesitated only a moment.

Clare tucked the sheet around her and let her eyes adjust to the dimness caused by twilight. She heard the purr of a zipper as Sam settled a pair of jeans on his hips. When he turned, she asked, "Where are you going?"

"Kitchen raid. I heard William come in a while ago. I'll go whip up a snack." Sam leaned over her and kissed her long and hard. "When I get back, we're going to have that talk."

Sam left the room and allowed himself to hope she'd come to terms with her past enough to admit the possibility of a future. She settled her differences with Ellie, which meant she was opening up. Smiling, Sam took the stairs two at a time.

Wine and cheese might be clichéd as a lover's feast, but it was quick and easy. So Sam grabbed a tray from the cabinet, slid it onto the table, and arranged his indoor picnic. In his hurry to get back to Clare, he scooped the tray off the table and knocked a pad onto the floor.

Muttering a curse, he set the tray back down. By the time he'd retrieved the pad, thoughts of an intimate conversation with Clare were gone. He tore the top sheet from the pad and stared at the list in his hand, a list that reduced human emotion to neatly penciled words. Words neatly penciled in Clare's handwriting.

Anger began to boil in the pit of Sam's stomach. She didn't trust him any more now than she did the day he met her. He told her he loved her, for God's sake! That wasn't something he said to make idle conversation. The hole in his life that had been shrinking suddenly opened wide and threatened to swallow him.

The title at the top of the page made him angrier than anything else on the list. He didn't care whether or not William was a plus *and* a minus. He didn't care that he got high marks because animals and children liked him. What he did care about was that she could write *Loving Sam* across the top of the page and then deliberately dissect the emotion.

Wine and cheese forgotten, Sam left the kitchen and walked slowly back upstairs to find Clare dressed and making the bed. Her bright smile faded as he held out the list and narrowed his eyes. Raw emotion resonated in his voice as he asked, "Do you trust anyone? I don't think so. You don't need a man, Clare. You need a boomerang, something you can't ever lose."

Stung by the anger in his voice and surprised at his reaction to her list, Clare retreated behind the control that had kept her safe for so long. She put up the wall that kept her from being hurt. Her defenses urged her to strike first, to reject him before he could finish rejecting her. Returning his volcanic gaze with an icy one, she said, "I never promised to change. That was your idea. You gambled. Gambles don't always pay off."

Crumpling the list, Sam said, "Are you so afraid of losing that you've forgotten how to feel instead of think? For God's sake, Clare! You made a list! You reduced your deepest emotions to logic."

"I make lists," she said quietly, unwilling to apologize for or explain the insecurity that resulted in the list. Defensively, she lifted her chin. "It's a habit."

"Habits won't wrap up your heart and keep you warm, Clare. Take a chance for once in your life."

Clare couldn't say anything. The man in front of her bore no resemblance to the casual man of the past few weeks. This man was angry, and she wasn't sure how to handle him. Even more important, she wasn't sure how to handle herself.

If love was supposed to be an inescapable conclusion, something felt in the soul, then why did she feel so uncertain of everything? Sam wanted her to give in to the fireworks, skyrockets, and the three words that would change her safe, secure life forever. She couldn't believe in them, couldn't take the risk, not when she thought that Sam was in love only with the idea of creating love.

Clare reached for the bedpost and curled her fingers around it, bracing herself. "Maybe I don't love you."

A cold knife slid into Sam's belly as he heard the fear behind her words, and he knew nothing he said would change Clare. He let silence drop between them before he finally spoke. "Maybe you're not capable of love, and maybe I've been wasting my time. I give up, so go back to your nice, safe little world, Clare, where you don't feel anything." Sam threw the wadded ball of paper to the ground and turned away. "You'll excuse me if I don't watch you pack."

The reverberation of the slamming door lingered in the room, filling her ears with the finality of Sam's parting words. Closing her eyes, Clare held her breath and fought back the tears. It was better this way. Better that she walk away before she got hurt any worse.

A half-sob, half-laugh escaped her. *What could hurt worse than this?* Sam didn't want her. Not unconditionally. Not the way she was. She'd lost count of the times she'd been sized up and put outside the circle. All her life she'd felt like a lonely child looking longingly in the pet store window. As if having a pet who loved her unconditionally would change the world.

It helped. At least she didn't have to face this alone.

Tears finally began to fall as she opened bureau drawers and tossed her clothes on the bed. She'd pack. She'd get out of Sam's house, out of his life, and maybe he'd get out of her heart. Clare looked at the mountain of personal belongings on the bed and whispered raggedly, "Now, where are those damned suitcases!"

As if on cue, William knocked on the door and called, "Miss Clare? Samuel said to fetch your suitcases."

Clare sniffed and rubbed a hand over her eyes before she crossed the room to open the door. "I'm . . . I'm leaving today."

Without words, William let her know he didn't think much of that idea. He huffed disgustedly as he brought the suitcases inside the room and hefted the largest one onto the bed.

Clare began stuffing the suitcases with her clothes. It was amazing how quickly she could pack if she didn't care about wrinkles or finding anything later. Being helpful, William began gathering the hanging clothes from the closet, which Clare took from him, folded once, and plopped in the suitcase.

"I don't believe I've ever seen Samuel in such a mood," William offered as though simply making idle conversation.

"Leave it alone, William," Clare gritted through her teeth as she tugged the zipper around the bulging suitcase. Then she carried the smaller bag to the bathroom and began throwing cosmetics into it.

As if he hadn't heard her, William continued. "That boy doesn't like to lose when he has his heart set on something."

"William," Clare warned again.

Her control was slipping and the tears were threatening again. She'd gone twenty-eight years without a kindly father figure giving her advice, and she hoped to God she could get out of that room without getting any advice now. Whether William lectured her, counseled her, or questioned her, the result would be the same—tears. She didn't want to cry in front of him.

"Done," she said firmly as she came out of the bathroom. "Could you take these downstairs? And bring my car up front?"

"Only woman I know that runs away from home with luggage," William muttered as he took the smaller bag from her. "I'll put these in your car, but Samuel's going to have to drag them back up here. I'm too old for this."

Her eyes burned with unshed tears. "I'm not coming back."

As he picked up the suitcases, William smiled kindly. "You're always welcome here. You remember that."

Clare swallowed the lump in her throat and nodded.

As William left, Clare exhaled the breath she'd been holding and looked around for Slick. "Come here, cat. I need you."

Fifteen minutes later, she finally managed to coax him from beneath the bed. "We're going back to the condo. It's just me and you again, Slick."

For a moment she nuzzled the fur at the base of his neck with her nose. All she wanted was to get out of the house before she saw Sam again. She didn't want to see him, notice the unruly blond hair she ached to tame with her fingers, or the way he looked at her with tobacco-brown eyes that promised forever.

Forever was for fools. She knew that.

Halfway down the hall, Slick began to push against her shoulders with his paws. He wiggled out of her arms, arrowing straight for Sam's bedroom. Clare caught her breath at the emotional punch delivered by Slick's defection. He'd chosen to stay with Sam, deserting her.

"Dammit," Clare whispered as tears threatened again. Even her cat didn't think she could love him. Fine. She didn't need any of them.

She practically ran outside to her car, but once she was behind the wheel, she couldn't make herself turn the key. Instead, she just sat there, bits and pieces of her conversation with William drifting through her mind.

Only woman I know that runs away from home with luggage.

William was right, she admitted to herself. She was running away from home. Away from the only home she'd known since she was seven years old. The condominium was familiar, but it wasn't home. Not anymore. Sam had seen to that. He'd taken her life and ripped it apart.

You're always welcome here.

"Not anymore, William, not anymore," she whispered as she let her head fall back against the seat. Sam had seen to that too. He wouldn't accept anything less than a total surrender of her heart. Sam wanted all of her—body and soul. He had wanted her to close her eyes and take a blind leap of faith. When she hesitated, he gave up on her. He walked away so easily.

I don't believe I've ever seen Samuel in such a mood.

William's observation made Clare's heart slam against her rib cage. He was right. Sam didn't walk away easily. Sam was furious. For the first time since she'd met Sam, he lost control. He yelled. He slammed a door. He hadn't debated her decision in a logical, dispassionate manner. This wasn't a game, not anymore.

Straightening and daring to hope, Clare felt some of the sadness lift. He *slammed* the door. Sam was smash-his-fist-into-the-wall angry. Suddenly all the doubts were gone.

Loving Sam wasn't her choice to make. Neither of them had a choice. He was as much a part of her now as her need to breathe. "God help me, I love you, Sam Tucker," she whispered as she got out of the car. No rockets or fireworks or bells accompanied her revelation, just an overwhelming certainty that she wanted the laughter and the joy and the passion she found with Sam to go on forever.

Bracing herself, she opened the front door and almost ran into Sam. He had Slick tucked under one arm and was reaching for the doorknob with the other. Both of them froze instantly, uncertain.

Sam broke the silence between them. "Here. I couldn't let you go without him. He's the one thing you love, and whether you know it or not, you need someone to love."

"I didn't come back for Slick," Clare said the words softly, willing him to understand everything those words represented. When Sam didn't answer, fear began to squeeze her heart.

The apprehension in her eyes both worried Sam and gave him hope. Everything he wanted, everything he dreamed since having Clare in his life seemed to shimmer just beyond his reach. So close and impossibly far away unless Clare had found the courage to love him. Sam carefully stepped out of the way so she could come all the way inside. As he shut the door, he ordered, "Say that again. Spell it out, Clare."

"I need someone to love, but I didn't come back for Slick. I came back because I don't want to be anywhere else."

Instantly, Sam dropped the cat and grabbed her shoulders. Blood roared in his ears as he tried to stop his heart from jumping to conclusions. "Why?"

Clare allowed herself a smile. "Because you slammed the door."

Sam backed her up against the wall, letting his hands rest on either side of her head. "What does my slamming doors have to do with anything?"

"You're in the same boat I am," Clare said as she looked up. "You don't have any more control over your emotions than I have over mine. You believe in forever, because it hurts too much if you don't."

Closing his eyes, Sam took a deep breath and let Clare slip into the hole in his life, filling it completely. "Say the words, Clare."

She lifted her face to press a kiss against his lips,

reveling in the warmth she knew she'd always find. "I love you, Sam Tucker. But you need to understand something about me."

"What don't I understand about you?"

Being honest wasn't easy for Clare, but she knew she had to say it. "I'm not very careful with the people I love. I keep losing them."

"Ah, Clare," Sam whispered. "You can't lose me. You're a part of me. Don't ever forget that."

As Sam cradled her head on his chest, William complained from the top of the stairs. "For heaven's sake, Samuel. Kiss the girl and ask her to marry us."

Sam sighed and said, "We can't fire him, but we may have to kill him."

"Not before he gives away the bride," she said, and without taking her eyes off of Sam, she asked, "Is that okay with you, William?"

"That'd be just fine. Now, kiss the girl, Samuel, and let's get this over with. I've got work to do."

Sam smiled. "You'd best go do it then. This could take awhile."

When he finally kissed her, Clare felt the promise of forever in the touch of his lips to hers.

THE EDITORS' CORNER

Passion and adventure reign in next month's LOVESWEPTs as irresistible heroes and unforgettable heroines find love under very unusual circumstances. When fate throws them together, it's only a matter of time before each couple discovers that danger can lead to desire. So get set to ward off the winter chill with these white-hot romances.

Helen Mittermeyer casts her spell again in **DIVINITY BROWN**, LOVESWEPT #782. They call him the black sheep of the county, a sexy ne'er-do-well who'd followed his own path—and found more than a little trouble. But when Jake Blessing comes asking for help from Divinity Brown, the curvy siren of a lawyer just can't say no! Helen Mittermeyer fashions an enthralling love story that transcends time.

Karen Leabo has long been popular with romance

readers for her fantastic love stories. So we're very pleased to present her Loveswept debut, **HELL ON WHEELS**, LOVESWEPT #783. A brash thrill-seeker who likes living on the edge isn't Victoria Holt's idea of the perfect partner for her annual tornado chase—but Roan Cullen is ready, willing, and hers! Roan revels in teasing the flame-haired meteorologist in the close quarters of the weather van, wondering if his fiery kisses can take this proper spitfire by storm. Will the forecast read: struck by lightning or love? Karen Leabo combines playful humor with sizzling sensuality in this fast-paced tale that you won't be able to put down.

Tensions run hot and steamy in Laura Taylor's **DANGEROUS SURRENDER**, LOVESWEPT #784. He'd thrown his body over hers as soon as gunfire erupted in the bank, but Carrie Forbes was shocked to feel passion mixed with fear when Brian York pulled her beneath him! The rugged entrepreneur tempts her as no man ever has, makes her crave what she thought she'd never know, but can she trust the sweet vows of intimacy when heartbreak still lingers in the shadow of her soul? Weaving a web of danger with the aphrodisiac of love on the run, Laura Taylor brilliantly explores the tantalizing threads that bind two strangers together.

Loveswept welcomes the talented Cynthia Powell, whose very first novel, **UNTAMED**, LOVESWEPT #785, rounds out this month's lineup in a very big way. "Don't move," a fierce voice commands—and Faline Eastbrook gasps at the bronzed warrior whose amber eyes sear her flesh! Brand Weston's gaze is bold, thrilling, and utterly uncivilized, but she can't let the "Wildman" see her tremble—not if she wants to capture his magnificent cats on film. Brand knows that staking his claim is reckless, but Faline has to be his. Cynthia Powell is the perfect writer for you if you love romance that's steamy, seductive, and more than a bit savage. Her sultry writing does no less than set the pages on fire!

Happy reading!

With warmest wishes,

Beth de Guzman

Shauna Summers

Beth de Guzman   Shauna Summers

Senior Editor   Editor

P.S. Watch for these Bantam women's fiction titles coming in April: **MYSTIQUE**, Amanda Quick's latest bestseller, will be available in paperback. In nationally bestselling romances from RAINBOW to DEFIANT, Patricia Potter created stories that burn with the hot and dark emotions that bind a man and woman forever; now with **DIABLO**, this award-winning, highly acclaimed author sweeps readers once more into a breathtaking journey that transforms strangers into soulmates. Finally, from Geralyn Dawson comes **THE BAD LUCK WEDDING DRESS**. When her clients claim that wearing this dress is just asking for trouble, Jenny Fortune bets she can turn her luck around by wearing it at her own wedding. But first, she must find herself a groom! Be sure to see next month's LOVESWEPTs for a preview of these exceptional novels. And immediately following this page, preview the Bantam women's fiction titles on sale *now!*

Don't miss these extraordinary books
by your favorite Bantam authors

On sale in February:

GUILTY AS SIN
by *Tami Hoag*

BREATH OF MAGIC
by *Teresa Medeiros*

IVY SECRETS
by *Jean Stone*

Who can you trust?

Tami Hoag's impressive debut hardcover, NIGHT SINS, revealed her to be a masterful spinner of spine-chilling thrills. Now she once more tells a tale of dark suspense in . . .

GUILTY AS SIN

The kidnapping of eight-year-old Josh Kirkwood irrevocably altered the small town of Deer Lake, Minnesota. Even after the arrest of a suspect, fear maintains its grip and questions of innocence and guilt linger. Now, as Prosecutor Ellen North prepares to try her toughest case yet, she faces not only a sensation-driven press corps, political maneuvering, and her ex-lover as attorney for the defense, but an unwanted partner: Jay Butler Brooks, bestselling true-crime author and media darling, has been granted total access to the case—and to her. All the while, someone is following Ellen with deadly intent. When a second child is kidnapped while her prime suspect sits in jail, Ellen realizes that the game isn't over, it has just begun again. . . .

"If I were after you for nefarious purposes," he said as he advanced on Ellen, "would I be so careless as to approach you here?"

He pulled a gloved hand from his pocket and gestured gracefully to the parking lot, like a magician drawing attention to his stage.

"If I wanted to harm you," he said, stepping closer, "I would be smart enough to follow you home, find a way to slip into your house or garage, catch you where there would be little chance of witnesses or interference." He let those images take firm root in her mind. "That's what I would do if I were the sort of rascal who preys on women." He smiled again. "Which I am not."

"Who *are* you and what *do* you want?" Ellen demanded, unnerved by the fact that a part of her brain catalogued his manner as charming. No, not charming. Seductive. Disturbing.

"Jay Butler Brooks. I'm a writer—true crime. I can show you my driver's license if you'd like," he offered, but made no move to reach for it, only took another step toward her, never letting her get enough distance between them to diffuse the electric quality of the tension.

"I'd like for you to back off," Ellen said. She started to hold up a hand, a gesture meant to stop him in his tracks—or a foolish invitation for him to grab hold of her arm. Pulling the gesture back, she hefted her briefcase in her right hand, weighing its potential as a weapon or a shield. "If you think I'm getting close enough to you to look at a DMV photo, you must be out of your mind."

"Well, I have been so accused once or twice, but it never did stick. Now my Uncle Hooter, he's a different story. I could tell you some tales about him. Over dinner, perhaps?"

"Perhaps not."

He gave her a crestfallen look that was ruined by the sense that he was more amused than affronted. "After I waited for you out here in the cold?"

"After you stalked me and skulked around in the shadows?" she corrected him, moving another step backward. "After you've done your best to frighten me?"

"I frighten you, Ms. North? You don't strike me

as the sort of woman who would be easily frightened. That's certainly not the impression you gave at the press conference."

"I thought you said you aren't a reporter."

"No one at the courthouse ever asked," he confessed. "They assumed the same way you assumed. Forgive my pointing it out at this particular moment, but assumptions can be very dangerous things. Your boss needs to have a word with someone about security. This is a highly volatile case you've got here. Anything might happen. The possibilities are virtually endless. I'd be happy to discuss them with you. Over drinks," he suggested. "You look like you could do with one."

"If you want to see me, call my office."

"Oh, I want to see you, Ms. North," he murmured, his voice an almost tangible caress. "I'm not big on appointments, though. Preparation time eliminates spontaneity."

"That's the whole point."

"I prefer to catch people . . . off balance," he admitted. "They reveal more of their true selves."

"I have no intention of revealing anything to you." She stopped her retreat as a group of people emerged from the main doors of City Center. "I should have you arrested."

He arched a brow. "On what charge, Ms. North? Attempting to hold a conversation? Surely y'all are not so inhospitable as your weather here in Minnesota, are you?"

She gave him no answer. The voices of the people who had come out of the building rose and fell, only the odd word breaking clear as they made their way down the sidewalk. She turned and fell into step with the others as they passed.

Jay watched her walk away, head up, chin out, once again projecting an image of cool control. She didn't like being caught off guard. He would have bet money she was a list maker, a rule follower, the kind of woman who dotted all her *i*'s and crossed all her *t*'s, then double-checked them for good measure. She liked boundaries. She liked control. She had no intention of revealing anything to him.

"But you already have, Ms. Ellen North," he said, hunching up his shoulders as the wind bit a little harder and spat a sweep of fine white snow across the parking lot. "You already have."

From beloved national bestseller

Teresa Medeiros

comes an enchanting new time-travel romance

BREATH OF MAGIC

"*Medeiros pens the ultimate romantic fantasy.*"
—Publishers Weekly

Arian Whitewood hadn't quite gotten the hang of the powerful amulet she'd inherited from her mother, but she never expected it to whisk her more than 300 years into the future. Flying unsteadily on her broomstick, she suddenly finds herself tumbling from the sky to land at the feet of Tristan Lennox. The reclusive Manhattan billionaire doesn't believe in magic, but he has his own reasons for offering one million dollars to anyone who can prove it exists.

Present-Day Manhattan

The media hadn't dubbed the four-thousand-square-foot penthouse perched at the apex of Lennox Tower "The Fortress" for nothing, Michael Copperfield thought as he changed elevators for the third time, keyed his security code into the lighted pad, and jabbed the button for the ninety-fifth floor.

The elevator doors slid open with a sibilant hiss. Resisting the temptation to gawk at the dazzling night view of the Manhattan skyline, Copperfield strode across a meadow of neutral beige carpet and shoved open the door at the far end of the suite.

"Do come in," said a dry voice. "Don't bother to knock."

Copperfield slapped that morning's edition of *The Times* on the chrome desk and stabbed a finger at the headline. "I just got back from Chicago. What in the hell is the meaning of this?"

A pair of frosty gray eyes flicked from the blinking cursor on the computer screen to the crumpled newspaper. "I should think it requires no explanation. You can't have been my PR advisor for all these years without learning how to read."

Copperfield glared at the man he had called friend for twenty-five years and employer for seven. "Oh, I can read quite well. Even between the lines." To prove his point, he snatched up the paper and read, " 'Tristan Lennox—founder, CEO, and primary stockholder of Lennox Enterprises—offers one million dollars to anyone who can prove that magic exists outside the boundaries of science. Public exhibition to be held tomorrow morning in the courtyard of Lennox Tower. Eccentric boy billionaire seeks only serious applicants.' " Copperfield twisted the paper as if to throttle his employer with it. "*Serious* applicants? Why, you'll have every psychic-hotline operator, swindler, and *Geraldo* reject on your doorstep by dawn!"

"Geraldo already called. I gave him your home number."

"How can you be so glib when I've faxed my fingers to the bone trying to establish a respectable reputation for you?"

Droll amusement glittered in Tristan's hooded eyes. "I'll give you a ten-thousand-dollar bonus if you can get them to stop calling me the 'boy billionaire.' It makes me feel like Bruce Wayne without the

Batmobile. And I did just turn thirty-two. I hardly qualify as a 'boy' anything."

"How long are you going to keep indulging these ridiculous whims of yours? Until you've completely destroyed your credibility? Until everyone in New York is laughing behind your back?"

"Until I find what I'm looking for."

"What? Or who?"

Ignoring Copperfield's pointed question, as he had for the past ten years, Tristan flipped off fax and computer with a single switch and rose from the swivel chair.

As he approached the north wall, an invisible seam widened to reveal a walk-in closet twice the size of Copperfield's loft apartment.

As Tristan activated an automated tie rack, Copperfield said, "Sometimes I think you flaunt convention deliberately. To keep everyone at arm's length where they can't hurt you." He drew in a steadying breath. "To keep the old scandal alive."

For a tense moment, the only sound was the mechanical swish of the ties circling their narrow track.

Then Tristan's shoulders lifted in a dispassionate shrug as he chose a burgundy striped silk to match his Armani suit. "Discrediting charlatans is a hobby. No different from playing the stock market or collecting Picassos." He knotted the tie with expert efficiency, shooting Copperfield a mocking glance. "Or romancing bulimic supermodels with Godiva chocolates."

Copperfield folded his arms over his chest. "Have you had my apartment under surveillance again, or did you conjure up that sordid image in your crystal ball? At least I give chocolates. As I recall, the last model I introduced you to didn't get so much as a 'thank you, ma'am' after her 'wham-bam.' "

Tristan's expression flickered with something that might have been shame in a less guarded man. "I meant to have my secretary send some flowers." He chose a pair of platinum cuff links from a mahogany tray. "If it's the million dollars you're worried about, Cop, don't waste your energy. I'm the last man who expects to forfeit that prize."

"Well, you know what they say. Within the chest of every cynic beats the heart of a disillusioned optimist."

Tristan brushed past him, fixing both his cuff links and his mask of aloof indifference firmly in place. "You should know better than anyone that I stopped believing in magic a long time ago."

"So you say, my friend," Copperfield murmured to himself. "So you say."

He pivoted only to discover that Tristan's exit had prompted the closet doors to glide soundlessly shut.

Copperfield rushed forward and began to bang on the seamless expanse with both fists. "Hey! Somebody let me out of here! Damn you, Tristan! You arrogant son of a—" A disbelieving bark of laughter escaped him as he braced his shoulder against the door. "Well, I'll be damned. What else can go wrong today?"

He found out an instant later when the mellow lighting programmed to respond solely to the mean average of his employer's heart rate flickered, then went out.

17th-Century Massachusetts

The girl plopped down on the broomstick. Her skirts bunched around her knees, baring a pair of slender calves shrouded in black stockings. A stray gust of wind rattled the dying leaves and ruffled her hair, forcing her to swipe a dark curl from her eyes. Gooseflesh prickled along her arms.

Shaking off the foreboding pall of the sky, she gripped the broomstick with both hands and screwed her eyes shut. As she attempted the freshly memorized words, a cramp shot down her thigh, shattering her concentration. She tried shouting the spell, but the broomstick did not deign to grant even a bored shudder in response.

Her voice faded to a defeated whisper. Disappointment swelled in her throat, constricting the tender membranes until tears stung her eyes. Perhaps she'd been deluding herself. Perhaps she was just as wretched a witch as she'd always feared.

She loosened the taut laces of her homespun bodice to toy with the emerald amulet suspended from a delicate filigree chain. Although she kept it well hidden from prying eyes and ignored its presence except in moments of dire vexation, she still felt compelled to wear it over her heart like a badge of shame.

"*Sacrébleu*, I only wanted to fly," she muttered.

The broomstick lurched forward, then jerked to a halt. The amulet lay cool and indifferent over her galloping heart.

Afraid to heed her own fickle senses, she slowly drew the gold chain over her head and squeezed the amulet. Leaning over the weather-beaten stick, she whispered, "I only wanted to fly."

Nothing.

She straightened, shaking her head at her own folly.

The willow broom sailed into the air and stopped, leaving her dangling by one leg. The stick quivered beneath her, the intensity of its power making the tiny hairs at her nape bristle with excitement.

"Fly!" she commanded with feeling.

The broom hung poised in midair for a shuddering eternity, then aimed itself toward the crowns of the towering oaks. It darted to a dizzying height, then swooped down, dragging her backside along the ground for several feet before shooting into another wild ascent.

She whooped in delight, refusing to consider the perils of soaring around a small clearing on a splintery hearth broom. The harder she laughed, the faster the broom traveled, until she feared it would surely bolt the clearing and shoot for the late-afternoon sky.

With a tremendous effort, she heaved herself astride the broom. She perched in relative comfort for a full heartbeat before the curious conveyance rocketed upward on a path parallel with the tallest oak, then dove downward with equal haste. The ground reached up to slam into her startled face.

She wheezed like a beached cod, praying the air would show mercy and fill her straining lungs. When she could finally breathe again, she lifted her throbbing head to find the broom lying a few feet away.

She spat out a mouthful of crumbled leaves and glared at the lifeless stick.

But her disgust was forgotten as she became aware of the gentle warmth suffusing her palm. She unfolded her trembling fingers to find the amulet bathed in a lambent glow. Her mouth fell open in wonder as the emerald winked twice as if to confirm their secret, then faded to darkness.

From the highly acclaimed author
of *First Loves* and *Sins of Innocence*

IVY SECRETS
by
Jean Stone

"Jean Stone understands the human heart."
—Literary Times

With a poignant and evocative touch, Jean Stone tells the
enthralling story of three women from vastly different
backgrounds bound together by an inescapable lie. They
were roommates at one of New England's most prestigious
colleges; now Charlie, Tess, and Marina are haunted by the
truth of the past, and the fate of a young girl depends on
their willingness to tell . . . Ivy Secrets.

She climbed the stairs to the fourth floor and slowly
went to her room. Inside, she sat on the edge of her
bed and let the tears flow quietly, the way a princess
had been taught. She hated the feeling that would not
go away, the feeling that there was another person
inside of her, wanting to spring out, wanting to be
part of the world. The world where people could talk
about their feelings, could share their hopes, their
dreams, their destinies not preordained. She hated
that her emotions were tangled with complications,
squeezed between oppressive layers of obligation, of
duty. Above it all, Marina longed for Viktor; she
ached for love. She held her stomach and bent for-

ward, trying to push the torment away, willing her tears to stop.

"Marina, what's wrong?"

Marina looked up. It was Charlie. And Tess.

"Nothing." She stood, wiped her tears. "I have a dreadful headache. And cramps." There was no way these two girls—blue-collar Charlie and odd, artsy Tess—would ever understand her life, her pain.

Tess walked into the room and sat at Marina's desk. "I hate cramps," she said. "My mother calls it the curse."

"I have a heating pad, Marina," Charlie said.

"Do you want some Midol?" Tess asked.

Marina slouched back on the bed. She could no longer hold back her tears. "It is not my period," she said. "It is Viktor."

Her friends were silent.

Marina put her face in her hands and wept. It hurt, it ached, it throbbed inside her heart. She had never—ever—cried in front of anyone. But as she tried to get control of herself, the sobs grew more intense. She struggled to stop crying. She could not.

Then she felt a hand on her shoulder. A gentle hand. "Marina?" Charlie asked. "What happened?"

Marina could not take her hands from her face.

"God, Marina," Tess said, "what did he do?"

She shook her head. "Nothing," she sobbed. "Absolutely nothing."

The girls were silent again.

"It's okay," Charlie said finally. "Whatever it is, it's okay. You can tell us."

"You'll feel better," Tess added. "Honest, you will."

Slowly, Marina's sobs eased. She sniffed for a moment, then set her hands on her lap. Through her watery eyes, she saw that Charlie sat beside her; Tess had moved her chair a little closer.

"He does not understand," she said. "He does not understand how much I love him." She stood and went to the window, not wanting to see their reactions. She yanked down the window shade. "There. I said it. I love Viktor Coe. I am in love with my damn bodyguard who doesn't give a rat's ass about me."

Charlie cleared her throat.

"Jesus," Tess said.

"I love him," Marina said. "And it is impossible. He is a bodyguard. I am a princess. Neither of you have any idea how that feels. You can fall in love with any boy you meet. It does not matter. The future of a country does not matter." She flopped back on the bed. Her limbs ached, her eyes ached, her heart felt as though it had been shattered into thousands of pieces.

"Does he know you love him?" Tess asked. "Have you told him?"

"There is no point. It would only cause more problems. Besides," she added as she hung her head. "He has someone else now. I have waited too long."

"He has someone else?" Charlie asked. "Here?"

"Yes," Marina said and cast a sharp glance at Tess. "Your friend, Tess. That woman. Dell Brooks."

Tess blinked. "Dell? God, she's my mother's age."

"Viktor is not much younger. He is in his thirties."

Tess blew out a puff of air. "Are you sure, Marina? I can't believe that Dell . . ."

"Believe it. I saw it with my own two eyes."

"Maybe they're just friends," Charlie said.

Marina laughed. "Americans are so naive."

"I think you should tell him," Tess said.

"I cannot."

"Yes, you can. The problem is, you won't."

Marina studied Tess. What could this teenage misfit possibly know? Or Charlie—the goody two-shoes who thought angora sweaters were the key to happiness?

"You won't tell him because you're afraid," Tess continued. "You're afraid he doesn't feel the same way about you, and then you'll be hurt."

"You sound like you know what you're talking about," Charlie said.

Tess shrugged. "It only makes sense. We may be naive Americans, but we know that hurt's part of life. Maybe Novokia-ites—or whatever you call yourselves —don't realize that."

Marina laughed. "I believe we are called Novoki-ans."

"Novokian, schmovokian. I think you should tell the man. Get it over with."

"You might be surprised at his reaction," Charlie agreed.

Marina looked at her closed shade. Viktor thought she was tucked in for the night, he thought she was safe. He had no idea that he was the one inflicting her pain, not the strangers that he anticipated were lurking behind every bush.

She turned to Charlie and Tess—her friends. This was, she reminded herself, part of why she had come to America. She had wanted friends. She had wanted to feel like a normal girl. Maybe Charlie and Tess were more "normal" than she'd thought. And maybe, just maybe, they were right.

"Will you help me?" Marina asked. "Will you help me figure out a plan?"

To enter the sweepstakes outlined below, you must respond by the date specified and follow all entry instructions published elsewhere in this offer.

DREAM COME TRUE SWEEPSTAKES

Sweepstakes begins 9/1/94, ends 1/15/96. To qualify for the Early Bird Prize, entry must be received by the ate specified elsewhere in this offer. Winners will be selected in random drawings on 2/29/96 by an indepen- nt judging organization whose decisions are final. Early Bird winner will be selected in a separate drawing om among all qualifying entries.

Odds of winning determined by total number of entries received. Distribution not to exceed 300 million.

Estimated maximum retail value of prizes: Grand (1) $25,000 (cash alternative $20,000); First (1) $2,000; cond (1) $750; Third (50) $75; Fourth (1,000) $50; Early Bird (1) $5,000. Total prize value: $86,500.

Automobile and travel trailer must be picked up at a local dealer; all other merchandise prizes will be ipped to winners. Awarding of any prize to a minor will require written permission of parent/guardian. If a ip prize is won by a minor, s/he must be accompanied by parent/legal guardian. Trip prizes subject to avail- ility and must be completed within 12 months of date awarded. Blackout dates may apply. Early Bird trip is n a space available basis and does not include port charges, gratuities, optional shore excursions and onboard ersonal purchases. Prizes are not transferable or redeemable for cash except as specified. No substitution for rizes except as necessary due to unavailability. Travel trailer and/or automobile license and registration fees re winners' responsibility as are any other incidental expenses not specified herein.

Early Bird Prize may not be offered in some presentations of this sweepstakes. Grand through third prize inners will have the option of selecting any prize offered at level won. All prizes will be awarded. Drawing will e held at 204 Center Square Road, Bridgeport, NJ 08014. Winners need not be present. For winners list (avail- ble in June, 1996), send a self-addressed, stamped envelope by 1/15/96 to: Dream Come True Winners, P.O. ox 572, Gibbstown, NJ 08027.

THE FOLLOWING APPLIES TO THE SWEEPSTAKES ABOVE:

No purchase necessary. No photocopied or mechanically reproduced entries will be accepted. Not responsi- le for lost, late, misdirected, damaged, incomplete, illegible, or postage-die mail. Entries become the property f sponsors and will not be returned.

Winner(s) will be notified by mail. Winner(s) may be required to sign and return an affidavit of eligibility/ elease within 14 days of date on notification or an alternate may be selected. Except where prohibited by law, entry onstitutes permission to use of winners' names, hometowns, and likenesses for publicity without additional com- ensation. Void where prohibited or restricted. All federal, state, provincial, and local laws and regulations apply.

All prize values are in U.S. currency. Presentation of prizes may vary; values at a given prize level will be pproximately the same. All taxes are winners' responsibility.

Canadian residents, in order to win, must first correctly answer a time-limited skill testing question admin- istered by mail. Any litigation regarding the conduct and awarding of a prize in this publicity contest by a resi- dent of the province of Quebec may be submitted to the Regie des loteries et courses du Quebec.

Sweepstakes is open to legal residents of the U.S., Canada, and Europe (in those areas where made avail- able) who have received this offer.

Sweepstakes in sponsored by Ventura Associates, 1211 Avenue of the Americas, New York, NY 10036 and presented by independent businesses. Employees of these, their advertising agencies and promotional compa- nies involved in this promotion, and their immediate families, agents, successors, and assignees shall be ineli- gible to participate in the promotion and shall not be eligible for any prizes covered herein.   SWP 3/95